The Hunting of
Lope Gamboa

Texas Rangers Jack Carson and Eddie Brand have been hunting outlaw Lope Gamboa for some time without success, but when they ride into Yuma it seems their luck has changed.

An assignment of US gold is to be transported along the Oxbow route by Conestoga wagon and the Rangers are convinced that Gamboa will attempt to steal the gold.

As all factions close in on the lumbering Conestoga wagon, the trail leads inexorably to a bloody climax in the Gila desert. . . .

The Hunting of Lope Gamboa

Jack Sheriff

A Black Horse Western

ROBERT HALE · LONDON

ISBN 978-0-7090-8925-4

Robert Hale Limited
Clerkenwell House
Clerkenwell Green
London EC1R 0HT

www.halebooks.com

Typeset by
Derek Doyle & Associates, Shaw Heath
Printed and bound in Great Britain by
CPI Antony Rowe, Chippenham and Eastbourne

PART ONE

PROLOGUE

They walked bare-headed through the heat with the sun beating down out of a searing white sky and the dust kicked up by their feet sticking to their moist skin and leaving an acrid touch and taste on their teeth. They walked fast but awkwardly on round-heeled cowboy boots, walking as if pursued by demons when behind them there was nothing but barren emptiness and the long slope up to the massive stone walls of the Yuma Penitentiary. The prison's huge oak doors, iron bound and studded, were closed. If the two men chose to look back – God forbid, one of them had sworn when the other cast a glance his way – it would have been the first time in five years that they had seen those doors from the outside.

'Your reputation arrived ahead of you,' Adam Kade said when, heads swimming, mouths bone dry, they pulled off the the trail and sank down in the shade under scrawny trees. 'When I heard I was getting out at the same time as Deakin Hood I didn't know whether to laugh or cry.'

'Praise the Lord would be a better reaction,' Hood said. 'In the days and months ahead you're going to need me.'

'Is that a fact? Are you saying I'm privileged to be with a man who lifted a rock above his head and brought it down to smash a prison guard's arm? A man who – so the story goes – preferred solitary confinement in the hole to the company of other men?'

'I'm choosy,' Hood said. 'Mixing with degenerates is not my style.'

Kade chuckled. 'Yeah, I can see how that would be a problem in a festering hell hole like Yuma Pen, but where does it put me?'

Hood was watching him with speculation.

'Breaking a prison guard's arm is as nothing when compared to smashing a chair over the prison governor's head in his own office – which I hear is what you did when you were up for parole.'

Kade shrugged. 'A serious mistake. Both of those acts should attract disbelief, not admiration. We blew it, Hood. Release for us both could have come in two years. Mindless violence meant we served the maximum term.'

'That makes us two of a kind. And to get what we want, we need each other.'

'That all depends,' Kade said, 'on what it is we want, and where we go from here.'

And suddenly he realized that by responding in that particular way he had not only accepted the truth in Hood's flat statement, but had put himself shoulder to shoulder with the big man. What was that down to? His own foolishness? The strength of the other man's personality? Or a recognition that on the outside he would struggle to survive on his own?

'They kicked us out with just a couple of dollars between us, so now we need just about everything we can lay our hands on,' Hood said, after a moment's thought. 'We need clothing, we need horses – we need weapons.'

'Weapons first,' Kade pointed out, 'because without an iron on our hip we're lions without teeth.'

Hood grinned. 'Sure. Two dollars won't buy what we need, so we must equip ourselves at the point of a gun.' He turned to gaze into the shimmering distance. 'Whatever we need, we need in a hurry – and the nearest town's Yuma. So, in part answer to your question, where we go from here is Yuma.'

'All right.' Kade nodded slowly. 'Look ahead fourteen hours. Now it's midnight. We're in Yuma, we're armed, we're clothed and fed and we're mounted on the best horses we could find—'

'You believe we can do all that?'

'Oh yes. And I've a pretty good idea what we're going to do when it's done. I don't know why you served time—'

'I was convicted of a murder I didn't commit.'

'I killed a man,' Kade said. 'My justifiable plea of self-defence was laughed out of court.'

Hood's slate-grey eyes had hardened.

'If we're both telling the truth we served five years without any justification. We were wrongfully incarcerated. The lawmen who arrested us and the judges who slammed us in the big stone hoosegow will get away with it. They always do. But they're small cogs in a big system headed by a man over there in Washington called Grover Cleveland.'

'The president. Are you proposing to take on the whole of the United States?'

'I'm about to begin nibbling away at the edges,' Hood said. 'There's too much money in that system, not enough in my pocket. I've got a number floating around in my head. That's the compensation I figure I've got coming to me for the time I spent in Yuma Pen. I know how to get it, where to get it, but right now—'

'Right now,' Adam Kade said, climbing to his feet and slapping at his dusty clothes, 'we both need a couple of drinks: one to quench a terrible thirst, the other to set us up for what lies ahead.'

ONE

It was midday when Texas Rangers Frank Carson and Eddie Brand took the Yuma Crossing over the Colorado River, their horses' hoofs rattling on the wooden bridge. They rode down into a town dozing in the oppressive heat. It would not come alive again until late afternoon, a situation which suited the rangers. After a two-week futile manhunt for a Mexican 'breed called Lope Gamboa that had taken them deep into Mexico then north into California they were ready for hot baths, close shaves and a meal of fried beef and eggs washed down with hot coffee. They had been dreaming of food that was cooked for them, didn't stink of camp-fire woodsmoke, and was on steaming plates placed before them on a table spread with a clean white cloth.

'Maybe too much to hope for,' Carson said, 'unless we book into Yuma's classiest hotel.'

'Already figured that out,' Brand said, 'which is why I'm looking for a greasy café – preferably one next door to a saloon. We came too close to ending up in a Mexican grave for my liking. I need something to put steel into my backbone before we continue the chase.'

'My priority is a talk with the town marshal. His name's Lars Sorensen. He rode in the army under Crook. That means he'll have clashed with Geronimo. Lope Gamboa once rode with Geronimo.'

'And you think Sorensen might know the 'breed's habits, his old stamping grounds, and could maybe give us some pointers?'

'It's a chance. Or maybe I'm looking for sympathy, someone to tell me Gamboa's a slippery customer, a cat with nine lives there's not a hope in hell of catching.'

Brand grinned. 'I'll put my horse in the town barn later. I advise you to do the same when you're finished with Sorensen. I don't care what that fellow comes up with, tonight I'm sleeping in a soft bed.'

'You've been wasting your time. Last I heard of Lope Gamboa, he was stealing horses from a ranch north of Gila Bend.'

'Dammit.'

A flimsy wooden chair was creaking a protest under Carson's big frame. His long legs were extended, his ankles crossed. A steaming cup of coffee was clasped in both hands. Fumes from the whiskey Lars Sorensen had splashed into the black java were strong enough to sting his eyes. He reached up, removed his dusty Stetson and dropped it on the floor at his side. With a yawn, he freed one hand and ran fingers through dark hair stiffened by days of desert riding in the hot sun.

He caught Sorensen watching him, and grinned ruefully.

'Yeah, a hot bath's high on the list of priorities. But first I need to pick your brains about Gamboa, this 'breed we've been hunting.'

Sorensen had his feet on the desk, his hands clasped behind his straggly grey hair. He was grimacing, as if mention of Gamboa had put a bad taste in his mouth.

'Gamboa's pure poison, a greaser who uses a knife to skin men alive. But I suppose you know that. He acquired rifles for the Indians, and for a time he rode with Geronimo. But his particular brand of treachery was too much for even the Apaches to stomach. When he saw them looking his way while sharpening their knives he slipped away from Geronimo's band to save his own swarthy skin.'

Carson sipped his coffee, thought back over what he knew.

'The rangers were after him for a string of atrocities committed against settlers in New Mexico when he was riding with a band of rogue Indians,' Carson said. 'Usual stuff, families slaughtered, buildings burnt down – but in one particular case a young boy went missing, presumed taken by that rogue band. This is going back some years, way before my time, and from what I've heard the rangers were at fault. They slipped up in some way. If they'd been sharper in reading signs that clearly spelled trouble, it's possible lives would have been saved, that boy never separated from his family.' He paused, frowning, then shrugged. 'More recently, Gamboa got into a gunfight on the Tex-Mex border. A Texas Ranger was shot in the back.'

Sorensen grunted. 'Which was like signing his own

death warrant. That killing made him a marked man.'

'It was known he'd then drifted north and west and fought with Geronimo and the Apaches in the Indian wars – which is back to what you've just confirmed. But then he disappeared, went off the map. Last year we picked up his scent again when his name was mentioned in connection with a bank raid in Tijuana.'

'And you went after him?'

'It was always a long shot. Distances are too great. There was also the problem of Gamboa's marksmanship. Anyone who'd met him could verify that he was just about the best long-range shot with a rifle they'd ever seen; for anyone hunting him that meant there was always the possibility of a bullet coming silently out of the blue and ending the chase. As it happened, I don't think we got close enough to him for even a long shot to be an option; me and my partner, we were chasing news that was always six months out of date.'

'Until now.'

Over the rim of his cup, Carson gazed hopefully at the Yuma marshal.

'That's right. So what's this about Gamboa stealing horses?'

Sorensen pulled a face, lazily uncrossed his ankles then crossed them in the other direction. Buying time to gather his thoughts, Carson judged, and suppressed a smile. How many times had he adopted the same tactic – particularly when tired?

'I must be getting old,' Sorensen said at last. 'My memory's playing tricks. I remember now, Gamboa was stealing horses, but when he'd got rid of them he moved on to do something much more interesting. You're from Texas, so you've maybe not heard of a band of Arizona outlaws headed by two Irish brothers, Bren and Mick Coogan?'

'I've heard the names. They've done nothing to get themselves into the history books.'

'Not yet they haven't. Tried to rob a couple of banks, without success, rustled some cows, sold stolen army rifles to the Apaches. But things could be about to change. Gamboa stealing those horses didn't raise eyebrows, but word was he then drifted south and joined up with the Coogans. Not earth-shattering news on its own, but Gamboa teaming up with those Irish hellions when a Conestoga wagon is due to pass this way with a heap of cash on board has made a lot of folk mighty jittery.'

'Cash?'

'From the California gold fields. Don't ask me what it's for. My guess is it's headed for Austin, or maybe all the way East to prop up Grover Cleveland's government.'

'And it's being carried by Conestoga wagon?'

'That's right. For some damn reason it's following the old Butterfield Overland Mail Trail – the Oxbow Route. Word I've got is it's being pulled by an eight-mule team. Wes Bates at the livery barn's got the job of tending to them when they stop over.'

'Wouldn't that cash be safer transported by railroad?'

'Faster, for sure. Safer? – well, nothing's ever one hundred per cent safe if there's someone out there wants it badly enough.'

'But it's not your concern, surely? Once that wagon's passed through Yuma it's not your responsibility.'

Sorensen spread his hands.

'I'm just answering your questions, feller. You mentioned Gamboa, he's linked to the Coogans, and with this gold shipment about due the rumours are thicker than flies over dead meat.'

Carson nodded slowly.

'Sure, and I thank you for that. Trouble is, it doesn't put us any closer to Gamboa. He joined the Coogans south of Gila Bend. If that Butterfield coach is crossing Arizona, the Coogans – and Gamboa – could hit it anywhere between Yuma and the border with New Mexico.'

'Always pleased to be of help to the Texas Rangers,' Sorensen said, and with a grin he raised his coffee cup to Frank Carson.

By ten that night, Eddie Brand was feeling pleasantly mellow. He knew that others watching him might have a different opinion – perhaps considering him as drunk as a lord. They would be wrong and, in Brand's learned opinion, not qualified to judge because a succession of full shot glasses swiftly upended had put them in exactly the same condition.

The saloon, at the upper end of Yuma's main street and standing tall alongside a ramshackle café, was almost empty. Working men had come and gone. Anyone counting customers would find he had spare fingers on one hand. The saloonist, thin and mournful, had been polishing the same glass for ten minutes.

The cow puncher standing next to Brand at the bar, a man called Seeger whom the ranger had befriended early in the evening, cocked an eyebrow.

'You see something funny?'

'Everything's funny, Seeg, but in partricular I find drunks expressing opinions about other drunks highly amusing.'

The 'puncher grinned. 'You said "partricular", Eddie. And nobody spoke, so which drunk's been expressing an opinion?'

'None in partricular,' Brand said, and he stared at Seeger with such a solemn face that the 'puncher burst out laughing.

'Eddie, my friend, I think it's time you called it a night.'

Brand shook his head. 'Texas Rangers never sleep.'

'I thought that was the Pinkertons? I could be wrong. Anyway, your partner's been and gone. By now he'll be snoring.'

'But others', Brand said, 'are just arriving,' and he nudged Seeger's elbow and nodded towards the door.

Two men had walked in from the street. And suddenly the room, already quiet, crackled with tension.

The first man in was over six feet tall and heavy with it, but walked with the grace of a dancer. The man behind him was shorter – though still tall – and if he had grace to match the bigger man's it was the balance and poise of a bare-knuckle fighter. Those characteristics were immediately apparent despite the men's obvious weariness. They were characteristics that spoke volumes about the men's strength and potential, yet the implication that there was violence in their make-up was weakened in one unusual way.

'No guns, no gun-belts,' Brand said softly, 'and no hats. What kind of men are these?'

'I'd say they're men recently released from the state penitentiary,' Seeger said. 'Looks like we're about to find out, because they're coming this way.'

TWO

The men with no hats and no guns walked across the sawdust together, but took up position at the bar on either side of Seeger and Eddie Brand. In the time it took them to do that, the other men in the saloon hastily drained their glasses and made for the street. When the door flapped behind the last man to leave, Seeger and Brand were alone with the new arrivals.

The saloonist hadn't moved. His face, however, had gone from mournful to grave, his eyes from distant to watchful.

From the saloonist the two big men ordered beer. They drank that first glass down in one long draught, and ordered a second. That swiftly followed the first. Then they put down their glasses and turned so that their backs were to the bar.

'I reckon you were thirsty,' Brand said, suddenly appreciating just how drunk he was. 'I guess it's been a long, hard day.'

'You could say that,' said the big man standing next to Brand. 'On the other hand, you could say a day's happenings are never clear until it's over – and this one's far from done.'

'Not a lot a man can do at night,' Seeger the cowman said, 'unless he's riding herd.'

The man alongside Seeger, the man with the poise of a bare-knuckle fighter, smiled pleasantly but spoke with menace.

'At night a man can act in a way that in daylight he'd find too risky, or just too damn dangerous,' he said.

And with a movement too swift for the eye to follow he slipped Seeger's six-gun from its holster and held it to the 'puncher's head. In the same movement he eased back the hammer with an oily snick. Cruelly, he twisted the pistol's butt, pressing with the heel of his hand. The ring of the muzzle bored into Seeger's temple.

The haggard, mournful saloonist stepped forward and banged down the glass he had been polishing to a jewel-like sheen. Suddenly his hands were below the level of the bar. His sunken eyes were as hard as agate.

'Enough,' he said, in a voice that rasped like dry gravel. 'Take your trouble out in the street, all of you, or I pull this trigger and cut someone in half.'

'You cut me in half, this boy here's dead,' said the man holding Seeger's pistol to its owner's head. He flashed a cruel grin. 'Could be he's dead anyway, unless we get instant co-operation.'

'We need horses, guns, and that cash you keep in a cigar box behind the bar.'

The big man standing beside Eddie Brand had spoken for the first time. His demands brought the saloonist's head around, narrowed his eyes. At the same time, with lazy efficiency, the big man dipped a hand and lifted Brand's six-gun from its holster.

Brand, feeling the hard liquor as a dull ache behind his eyes, reacted without thinking. He felt the pistol catch leather as it was lifted. Heard the snick as the big man tugged it free. Felt the sharp contact with cold steel as the foresight hit his elbow on the way up. Then he spun on heel and toe. He whipped his right arm backwards at waist level. His elbow drove like a piston into the big man's belly.

It was like hitting ridged oak. The big man took a light step backwards, up on his toes. Brand waited for him to fall, then looked at him in disbelief as he sucked in a deep breath and shook his head in obvious amusement. Out of the corner of his eye Brand saw the pistol flick away from the man's side. But now the strong drink was weighing heavily in his limbs. Warning bells rang. A belated signal left his brain. Before hands could lift to parry the blow or legs carry him out of danger, the pistol struck. Glittering in the weak lamplight, it cracked against the side of Brand's head.

Weak lamplight became sheet lightning, flaring in his brain. Then darkness descended.

'Here's the way it works.'

The man pressing Seeger's pistol to the 'puncher's temple eased the heel of his hand off the weapon, put a knuckle under Seeger's chin and lifted his head so that their gazes locked.

'You listening to this?'

'Listening,' Seeger said huskily.

'And you, behind the bar?'

The saloonist nodded.

'All right. First, introductions. My name's Adam Kade. The big man who got a mite overzealous with his shooting iron and downed your friend is Deakin Hood. Remember those names. Make sure when this episode's over the law in Yuma knows exactly who they're up against. You might phrase your telling as a warning: let them know that Kade and Hood are names that, in the months to come, will be spoken in hushed tones around Arizona camp-fires.'

Behind the bar, the saloonist listened with contempt to this flowery oratory, then turned his thin face to one side to spit drily.

Kade's grin was bleak.

'You just bought yourself a slice of pain, my friend. But before we get to that, as proprietor of this miserable joint, you have the honour of working for me. First, you empty the bills and coins from that cigar box onto the counter. Next, very carefully, you bring the shotgun out from under the bar and place it alongside the money. Then you come around the bar. You unbuckle these two bozos' gun-belts – and place those on the bar. You take off their hats – put them in the same place. After that' – he grinned across at his watching sidekick – 'the action moves outside so's we can look over some prime horse flesh.'

Deakin Hood was standing away from the bar, Brand's six-gun dangling loosely in one big fist. Ignoring the pistol held fast against his head, Seeger half turned and squinted sideways at the big man.

'The fellow you knocked down is a Texas Ranger. He needs a doctor. He's concussed, and he's not breathing right. If he dies,' Seeger said, 'your next trip to Yuma Pen will end at the gallows.'

'So, tell the skinny old-timer behind the bar to get his finger out of his ear—'

Hood broke off. His head jerked around. His eyes snapped towards the bar. The saloonist was already moving, apparently acting on Kade's instructions. He had taken one pace back to the shelves under the big mirror and picked up the cigar box he used for his takings. As he turned with it, he stumbled. The box tipped in his hand. Several coins spilled out. They hit the floor, jingling, rolling.

Muttering, the saloonist slammed the box on the bar, then ducked down. He kept his left hand flat on the box. The top of his head, laced with thin strands of black greasy hair, glistened in the lamplight.

For a brief moment he remained still. Then he straightened up with remarkable speed. He had a sawn-off shotgun in his right hand. Somehow he'd cocked it. He swung it horizontally across the bar. His bony finger was hooked around the double triggers.

Hood, the big man, froze.

Kade again moved like greased lightning. The blued barrels of the shotgun swung towards him in a glittering arc. The twin muzzles gaped. He was staring into yawning black holes loaded with death. The saloonist's knuckle gleamed white.

Kade whipped the pistol away from Seeger's head.

He sprang forward and slammed a hand flat on the bar. His feet left the floor. Leaning at full stretch, he brought the pistol up and over. He put his full weight into the vicious downward swing. The pistol's barrel glanced off the side of the saloonist's head and smashed down on his shoulder. His scalp split. Blood cascaded, soaking his shirt, turning the side of his face into a glistening red mask. There was a sickening crack as his collarbone splintered. His eyes rolled. He fell backwards.

There was a tremendous roar as his finger involuntarily tightened on the trigger. The double shotgun blast punched a huge hole in the big mirror. Shards of glass flew in a glittering shower of razor-sharp shrapnel, pinging off the hanging lamps.

Ears ringing, vision blurred by the shotgun's mighty muzzle flash, Seeger instinctively ducked. He flung an arm across his face to protect his eyes. Behind him, Deakin Hood had fallen back uttering a string of foul curses.

Adam Kade had attacked the saloonist to save his own life, but was paying the price for having over-extended himself.

Forward momentum kept him spread-eagled across the bar. As the saloonist sank groaning to the floor, the pistol's unstoppable downward swing threatened to pull Kade down on top of him.

Seeger pounced.

With both hands he grabbed the back of Kade's shirt. Then he put one knee against the front of the bar and heaved. Kade came sliding back across the timber surface. Seeger heard his chin hit the far edge of the bar. His teeth snapped shut. Then, fingers still locked, Seeger dragged him all the way back across the bar and flung him bodily to the floor. As Kade hit the sawdust-covered dirt floor, face down, Seeger stamped on his wrist. Kade roared in agony. The pistol fell from his fingers.

Seeger dropped to one knee, reaching across Kade for the six-gun. From out of the dim light, a boot came swinging. The toe caught Seeger flush on the side of the jaw. A tooth snapped. Blood pooled in his mouth. He was knocked bodily sideways. With both hands, he broke his fall, tried to roll clear. But Hood had followed him relentlessly. A second powerful kick landed on the bony protrusion behind Seeger's ear. His muscles turned to water. He flopped onto his side. Voices blurred, suddenly reduced to an indistinct buzz that seemed to come and go, swell then recede.

Deakin Hood stepped away from Seeger. Strangely fastidious, he stood on one leg to wipe the toe of his boot on the back of his pants.

Adam Kade said, 'That shotgun blast will have roused the whole town, the marshal will be on his way up the street. We've got minutes to get the hell out of here and you've gone squeamish—'

'Grab the money.'

Kade shook his head in disbelief and ran to the bar. He emptied the cigarette box, stuffed notes and coins into his pockets as he ran around behind the bar. From beneath it he grabbed boxes of cartridges for the shotgun. Then he bent and scooped up the deadly weapon.

Hood was down on his knees alongside Seeger. He'd rolled the 'puncher onto his back. Now he unbuckled his gun-belt and stripped it from the half-conscious man's waist, and gestured to Brand. Kade stuffed the ammunition inside his shirt, then dropped down and removed the ashen-faced Eddie Brand's gun-belt.

'Let's go.'

Wearing the stolen Stetsons, buckling stolen gun-belts around their waists, the two men ran for the door. They burst out into the night air. And suddenly they could hear excited voices.

Fifty yards down the street, a man was running hard in their direction. He was brandishing a pistol and calling over his shoulder. Behind him light flooded from an open doorway.

There were two horses at the hitch rail. The shotgun blast had spooked them. They were bolt upright and quivering, eyes rolling white, ears flattened. Without hesitation, Kade and Hood took one apiece, flicked the reins loose and flung themselves into the saddle. The excited horses needed little encouragement. Acutely aware of the man running up the street, sensing danger in the glittering weapon carried in his fist, they wheeled away from the hitch rail. In ten bounding strides they were at full gallop.

With the cries of the frustrated lawman ringing in their ears, Adam Kade and Deakin Hood hammered up Yuma's main street and tore out of town.

THREE

'Less than fifty-fifty. He's in a coma. If you can tell me when he's going to come out of it you're welcome to my job.'

Doctor John Hall was a rotund character of indeterminate age who wore wire glasses perched on the very tip of a podgy nose. The buttons of a linen coat that had once been white were being tested by his substantial girth. His grey eyes were wise, but unhelpful. He had a habit of running fingers across a scalp where reddish hair had once flourished.

He was standing with Frank Carson and Marshal Lars Sorensen. The room was dimly lit. All three men were peering down at the still form of Eddie Brand. The unconscious ranger lay on a cot in the shadows, his body covered by a thin sheet. His head was bandaged. His closed eyelids were almost blue against his deathly white face.

Seeger, the cowpoke who had been involved in the saloon fracas, was sitting on a stool with his back against the wall, stripped to the waist. Purple blotches at various points on his anatomy showed where he had been daubed with strong antiseptic. In Frank Carson's voiced opinion, he stank like a recently dipped sheep.

With a sigh, Carson shook his head, turned away from his injured partner and looked across at Seeger.

'Adam Kade and Deakin Hood – have I got that right?'

'You got it.'

'They walked into the saloon, their stated intention to avail themselves of weapons, horses and so forth – and they went ahead and did just that?'

'That they did. And when they weren't kicking or pistol whipping everyone within range, they were insisting the marshal here be made aware of their names.'

Sorensen pulled a face.

'No hopers. Fresh out of the pen. They hightailed soon as they caught sight of me. It's unlikely they'll be heard of again in these parts.'

'That's not the picture they painted,' Seeger said. 'I think they're trouble.'

'I've already got trouble coming in the shape of a Conestoga wagon pulled by eight goddamn mules,' Sorensen said. 'When I've seen that on its way I'll maybe have time to worry about two ex-cons looking for excitement.'

'Unless there's a connection here,' Carson said.

Sorensen flashed him a glance.

'The Conestoga?'

'Most people know about it. I guess it's been in the newspapers' – Sorensen nodded – 'and I guess those newspapers find their way up to the jail.'

'True, but I'll tell you something else,' Sorensen said. 'It's not been mentioned anywhere that I know of, but it goes back to what we were talking about: the apparent foolhardiness of transporting cash overland in a wagon.'

Carson at once saw what the marshal was driving at.

'You reckon there'll be an escort?'

'Man, there has to be. When that wagon comes through Yuma it'll have a troop of United States Cavalry riding along with it; if it's a covered wagon, there'll be armed troopers inside. You mark my words, if Kade and Hood make a try for that cash they'll be back inside so fast they'll think they never left – or else they'll be very, very dead.'

It was well past midnight when Frank Carson returned to his room in the hotel. A bruised Seeger had ridden painfully out of town, heading for the home ranch. Doc Hall had retired to his bed, assuring Carson that he would look in on Eddie Brand at regular intervals and let Carson know at once if the injured ranger recovered consciousness.

The look in the kindly, balding doctor's eyes, Carson recalled gloomily, had not inspired confidence.

Contemplating a future without the man who had been his companion on the trail for more years than he cared to count, had stood back-to-back with him in enough gun fights to give him the permanent shakes, Carson sat on the edge of his bed, dug a flat bottle of whiskey from under the pillow and helped himself to a generous swig.

The strong spirit hit him hard. He coughed, rubbed his knuckles across watering eyes, then stood up and walked to the window. He was looking down on Yuma's main street. The saloon was directly across the street, Sorensen's office and jail away to his right. Oil lamps glowed in both windows. Sorensen, he knew, would be writing a record of the night's event's. The wife of the injured saloonist – who had been tended to then tenderly placed in his own bed – would probably be staring into space and sadly wondering at the wickedness of men and the wisdom of setting up business within sight of a state penitentiary.

Which, Carson decided, inevitably brought him back to the problem of Lope Gamboa.

When first he'd spoken to Lars Sorensen, it seemed that he and Brand were at last closing in on the savage 'breed with an unholy penchant for skinning knives. But Sorensen had been slow in coming up with precise details. When he did – or when he enlarged on what little he knew – Lope Gamboa had suddenly acquired dangerous sidekicks, and perhaps become involved in a lawless enterprise that could put him beyond the reach of Carson: any theft of government money would be dealt with by federal lawmen.

In the circumstances, that was to be regretted. Those circumstances were the critical condition of Texas Ranger Eddie Brand.

As he returned to his bed and stretched out with his hands behind his bed, anger was simmering within Frank Carson. Kade and Hood must pay for the attack on Brand. Trouble was, if the two ex-cons went after the government cash, then, like Lope Gamboa, they could be spirited away by federal lawmen to a place out of Carson's reach.

That, Carson thought grimly, was not going to happen. It was not going to happen in the case of Lope Gamboa; it was not going to happen in the case of Adam Kade and Deakin Hood.

Yet, as he at last drifted off to sleep with the dim light from the street's oil lamps seeping through the flimsy muslin curtains, Frank Carson was tormented by the realization that, unless he moved fast, he could lose all three men.

Make that four, was his final thought: Brand could go too.

FOUR

Both men were out of their blankets at first light, the ruddy glow from the eastern skies casting long shadows across the Arizona landscape and washing their dark tangled hair and unshaven faces with colour. They were camped twenty miles from Yuma, on the north bank of the Gila River. Shivering a little in the cool morning air, they sat close to the smokeless camp-fire eating jerky washed down with bitter coffee.

They had each been handed a few coins when they left the penitentiary. With that money they had walked into a Yuma general store and bought enough supplies to keep them alive, in the words of a stone-faced warden, *until they found work*. But, as Hood had boasted to his companion when they walked away from the grim stone building that for so long had been their home, he had other, bigger ideas.

As Adam Kade scrubbed his hands clean with coarse sand, he was watching Hood with interest. The big man had pulled a folded piece of newspaper out of his back pocket. As Kade watched, he unfolded it and carefully smoothed it on his thigh.

'That it?' Kade said.

'Is that what?'

'When we got to talking about this and that on the way down from the jail you said you'd figured out the compensation for the time you'd served, knew how to get it, where to get it—'

'The time *we'd* served,' Hood cut in. 'You're in this too, friend, up to your neck after last night's fun and games.'

'Maybe. I went along because west of the Mississippi there are certain items a man must have if he's going to stay alive. Last night's events provided what we need: we've got horses, we've got weapons. But that puts both of us in the happy position of being able to choose what we do next. I'm waiting to hear this big idea before I decide to tag along a while longer, or go it alone.'

'Without me—'

'Give it a rest,' Kade said. 'Yesterday you said we needed each other. That tells me what you've got planned can't be done by one man.'

'It can,' Hood said, 'but it would be risky. I know a man who could do it, would do it, all by himself. I've ridden with him, he's a renegade, a 'breed with a reputation. The sight of him and the knife he carries and wields with deadly results can make strong men weak at the knees.' Hood shrugged. 'Unfortunately, he moves around and I've been out of touch for five years. That being the case, I'm stuck with you—'

'Spit it out. If that's a vote of confidence, I need to know more about this big deal.'

Hood flexed his massive shoulders.

'Today's 1 June. According to this article in here, on 2 June a lone Conestoga wagon's due to take the Yuma crossing, drive on through the town and continue along the old Oxbow route across Arizona.'

'You figuring on starting your own haulage business with one stolen wagon?'

'It's not the wagon, it's what's in it.'

'Which is?'

'Cash.'

Kade frowned. 'A Conestoga wagon loaded with *money?*'

'According to this.' Hood tapped the crumpled paper.

'Doesn't make sense. If it's true, why tell the whole world? An undertaking like that needs secrecy. Bandits get wind of it, that money's as good as gone – and bandits *will* get wind of it because it's there in that goddamn newspaper.'

'A clever *reporter* got wind of it,' Hood said. 'A scoop like this could secure a get-up-and-go journalist a position on Joseph Pulitzer's *New York World* newspaper. This feller's going for it, and hang the cost to whoever's the brains behind this Conestoga caper.'

'All right, how about this: if money's being transported across Arizona, there'll be an armed escort.'

'Not mentioned here.'

'Take my word for it.'

'I don't have to, because this is the way we'll play it – if you're in.'

'Keep talking.'

'We set it up so we're in a position to take that money

34

and ride away – if the circumstances are favourable. If they're not – if you're right and I'm wrong and there is an armed escort too big for us to handle – we ride away anyway, only without the money. We try, we fail, but in the end we lose nothing.'

'But if I'm wrong and you're right and that wagon's there for the taking,' Adam Kade said softly, 'we stand to gain a fortune.'

Hood grinned. 'Sweet, isn't it? If we get in first. Before all those bandits standing in line for a slice of a very big cake.'

Kade frowned, thinking hard.

'So this wagon takes the Yuma crossing – then what? Across the Gila Desert to Gila Bend?'

'The Oxbow route's all I know.' Hood shrugged. 'I don't know details. I do know Butterfield's Concord coaches driving the Oxbow called at El Paso and Fort Smith on the way, but Lord knows how they got there.'

'OK. So, if we're going to do this, and the wagon's retracing an old route we're unfamiliar with, we go to the one place we know for sure it's going to be. Tomorrow morning we ride down, pick a spot on the eastern outskirts of Yuma. Then we wait, and watch. When the wagon comes through, we follow at a distance, then hit hard at the first favourable spot: that means clear of town, away from other habitation, not overlooked.'

'Not just the first favourable spot, but also at the most favourable time,' Hood said. 'That wagon will be slow moving. We follow it until darkness. *Then* we hit it.'

'That's what I had in mind,' Kade said.

Hood was grinning.

'See what I mean? We put our heads together, work together, we're going to ride away from this two very rich men.'

'Not ride,' Kade said, shaking his head. 'Can you see a haul of money this size being taken away in a couple of saddle-bags? No, Hood, a wagonload of money needs a wagon to transport it when it's stolen, and we haven't got one.'

'Good point. So we take the Conestoga—'

'No. We do that they'll track us as easy as tracking a black sheep across a snowfield.'

'Right again. OK, we got ourselves horses and guns, and by God we'll get ourselves a wagon in exactly the same way,' Deakin Hood said, climbing to his feet. He dragged out a battered turnip watch, consulted it and said happily, 'We'll steal one, Kade – and we've got a full twenty-four hours to do it in.'

It was Adam Kade who suggested they ride north towards the Castle Dome Mountains and, with the decision made, they broke camp when the early morning sun was already hot on their shoulders. It was impossible to remove all the signs of their overnight stay but, as Hood pointed out, if there were pursuers riding out of Yuma they would learn nothing of value from the cold ashes of a camp-fire and a few indistinct hoofprints on the banks of the Gila.

The landscape was typical desert, a stony emptiness baked by the sun, with distance always made confusing by the heat-haze that shimmered for most of the long days. As they pushed slowly north, that monotony was broken when the land began to rise and before them there stretched the sprawling foothills of Castle Dome. Here, too, there was more vegetation. In those south-western desert regions even a slight change in altitude brought with it a change in temperature. Cooler air meant moisture. Trees began to flourish, and arroyos and canyons became broad green fissures cutting deep into the soaring slopes.

It was Hood who spotted the buildings, tucked inside a fertile canyon, nestling in a stretch of trees blanketing much of the eastern slope.

'Ranch over there,' he said.

The two men drew rein.

Kade, who was riding Texas Ranger Eddie Brand's horse, reached back into the saddle-bag for the field-glasses he had discovered. After a moment's silent inspection of the distant buildings, he removed the glasses from his eyes and looked at Hood with a peculiar expression on his face.

'Deserted. No signs of life. Buildings are falling down—'

'So we push on,' Hood said.

'—but unless my eyes playing tricks on me,' Kade said, 'when the owner walked away he left equipment that could be of use to us.'

'Are you saying there's a wagon there?'

'That's exactly what I'm saying,' Kade said.

It was Hood's carefully considered opinion as they jogged lazily into the canyon that the wagon, when they got close enough to examine it, would be as derelict as the rest of the property. Quietly amused, Kade listened to the big man and knew he was talking that way to avoid tempting fate.

The amusement was soon wiped from his face, and from his mind.

They rode under a board once affixed to a couple of tall pole uprights on either side of the approach track, now sagging precariously from one of them. It announced, in letters seared into the rough pine with a red-hot branding iron, that they were entering La Buena Tierra. But the good land, whatever it had once been, was now a stony yard surrounded by decline, and ruin.

After a moment's hesitation, the two men swung out of the saddle.

The house was to the north. Most of the glass in its windows was missing or cracked. Its shingle roof had caved in. The gallery running around three sides sagged on broken posts so that its warped and splintered boards were half-hidden in overgrown grass. To the east, a tall barn with ruined walls was now open on two sides exposing a full-length loft. Remnants of bone-dry hay fluttered in the hot breeze. At the side of the barn a corral extended out to the west. Several poles had fallen. The gate leaned drunkenly from a broken rope hinge.

'This place,' Hood said quietly, 'has been in use.'

Kade nodded. There was the faint smell of woodsmoke. The hard-packed dirt yard bore the scuffed signs of perhaps half-a-dozen horses. He dropped to one knee, used a stick to poke into a mound of horse droppings.

'No more than a couple of hours old.'

'Goddamn it.'

'Hold on a minute,' Kade said, standing and putting a restraining touch on the big man's arm. 'By the looks of it, this place has been a long time deserted. Someone's been here – but they're not here now. Whoever it was, they won't have been the first, and they won't be the last – we're here to prove that. So there is no problem. Travellers use this place on their way through to somewhere else. They come, they go. Now it's our turn.'

Hood took a deep breath.

'I hope to God you're right. If you are, I can't think of a better place to use as a base. We use it today, and we use it when we return here tomorrow night with that wagon over there groaning under the weight of all that money.'

'If,' Kane said with caution. 'If it moves. If it's got spokes on the hubs, rims on the spokes. If its axles are not seized, rusted. The one thing we know won't be of any use are rotted traces, harness. But we can work that out, find something here, rope, rawhide—'

'The tongue's broken but the single- and double-trees are OK so we can hitch up the horses. As for the rest. . . .'

It moved.

Eagerly, both men rushed over to the old farm wagon. They put their shoulders to its sun-bleached timber and they pushed. And it moved. It moved with a creak, and a groan, as if protesting at the disturbance. But Kane and Hood, straining every muscle, moved it a yard, then they moved it ten, then another ten. And then they straightened, removed their stolen Stetsons and used the sleeves of their prison-issue shirts to wipe their streaming brows.

'In that barn over there,' Kane panted, 'the sun's shining on metal drums. Pound to a pinch of salt, that's axle grease.'

'We've got two horses to pull that thing. It'll be tough enough empty; fully laden. . . .'

'I'll have it running like new.'

'I've been thinking,' Hood said, leaning back against the wagon. 'We've roughed out a plan to steal a heap of cash – this wagon's a part of it – but before we take the next big step it's time to ink in the details.'

'What details? We latch on to the wagon when it leaves Yuma, we follow it, darkness falls and we move in. Isn't that enough?'

'No. We know we slip away into the shadows if there's an armed escort. But if there's no escort, the robbery goes ahead. How do we deal with the wagon driver?'

'And the man that's always going to be there riding shotgun.' Kade shrugged. 'I took a shotgun and shells away from that saloonist. We've both got six-guns—'

'If we're caught,' Hood cut in, 'robbery puts us back inside. I think I could handle that. Just. But murder's different. Murder gets us the gallows. Which is the one big reason I'm thanking the Lord that friend of mine I mentioned—'

'Which friend is that?'

'Never mind. I mentioned him at the campsite, said he could do what we're planning all on his own. But he'd do it the brutal way, a way that would end in murder. I don't want that, because if we're caught—'

'We won't be caught.'

Hood shook his head. 'Can you guarantee that?'

'Nobody can.'

'Exactly. So here's those details I was talking about. We follow that Conestoga wagon, but when the afternoon draws on we go past it. We touch our hats, we say our howdys, we ask them if they've never heard of the railroad – and we pull away; easy done, we're empty, that wagon's fully laden. A ways down the trail, when it's just about dusk – around the time when they'll be thinking of stopping for the night but haven't yet done so – we pull up and we put this old wagon broadside across the trail.'

'And wait.' Kade nodded. 'They stop, we've got the drop on them. If they've got sense, they throw down their weapons.'

'You like it?'

'It's perfect. Now will you stop worrying, big man?'

'Worrying?' Deakin Hood, clearly immeasurably relieved, threw back his head and roared with laugher. 'Yesterday at around this time I was worrying that there'd be a last minute hitch, and I'd never get out of jail. Today I'm worrying about money, more than any one man's seen in a lifetime, and what I'm going to do when I get my hot hands on it. I call that a change for the better.'

'Don't you mean when *we* get our hands on it?' Kade said.

Deakin Hood raised his eyebrows in mock surprise.

'Isn't that what I said?'

And then he winked broadly at Adam Kade, turned and walked towards the barn.

FIVE

Five miles to the south and east of the ruined ranch known as La Buena Tierra, three men rode out of the scorching desolation of the desert and allowed their thirsty horses to choose their own path across the sloping green banks of the Gila River. As the horses dipped their muzzles into the cool waters, ripples widening as they drank deeply, the three men slapped dust from their clothes with Stetsons stained with sweat and squinted into the dazzling sunlight.

One of the men pointed wordlessly to the remains of a camp-fire, hoofprints deeply indented in the soft earth. The others glanced over then shrugged, dismissing the signs of human presence as of no consequence. With a jingling of bridles and spurs they crossed the river where it was broad and shallow and rode up the south bank with water cascading from the horses' glistening coats.

'We rest here,' said Bren Coogan.

'Rest?' His brother, Mick, pushed back his hat and grinned. 'Let's say we're regrouping. There'll be no rest until this business is over. And even then there'll be none, for by tomorrow night the whole damn country will be after us for what we've done.'

'And isn't that a fine position to be in?' Bren said. 'We'll be running ahead of the pack, carrying with us enough money to make Grover Cleveland himself turn green with envy.'

'It's supposed to be Cleveland's money,' Mick said.

Bren winked. 'Isn't it almost poetic in its sheer beauty?'

The third member of the group, a swarthy man with glittering eyes, had kept silent and to one side. This man wore a flamboyant sombrero of faded reds and yellows, with a neck cord of woven silk that hung loose under his dark unshaven chin. His black hair was streaked with grey, his age somewhere between forty and sixty. One eyelid drooped. A knife had shaped a corner of his mouth; beneath a drooping black moustache his lips held a permanent, cynical sneer. From a worn saddle boot a shotgun jutted. On one hip he wore a six-gun; on the other a broad-bladed knife was carried in a beaded sheath with a leather fringe.

'It's a fine position to be in,' he said now, 'if we get there. But maybe to do that we need the luck of the Irish. A wagon is transporting money across open country. The men behind it will be experiencing fear and apprehension. That will create in them the need for extreme caution. They will make sure that money is guarded. If the wagon has an armed escort, many soldados bearing many guns, we will need that luck and much more if we are to succeed.'

Bren Coogan swung down, slapped his horse and watched it trot away into the lush grass and begin to graze. Mick Coogan followed suit. They walked away into the stand of twisted cottonwoods, followed by the man in the sombrero who dismounted and crossed the grass with lithe grace.

The three men seemed to breathe collective sighs of relief as they walked out of the searing sun and sank down in the thin shade. They rested their backs against the boles of the trees. The two Irishmen lit cigarettes, momentarily closing their eyes in pleasure.

'I couldn't believe it when Lope Gamboa came to us with a proposition,' Bren Coogan said in an offhand manner. 'Now I'm baffled. He said he would make us rich, but suddenly he's beset by doubts.'

Gamboa spat. He had lit a slim black cheroot. Blue smoke curled around long, greasy black hair, for he had removed his sombrero and tossed it to one side. His six-gun holster he had pulled around for comfort; it rested in his groin.

'Talk to me when you mention my name, not through your brother,' he said. 'There is no doubt. Gamboa does not understand the meaning of doubt. What he understands is the power of the knife and the gun. When I heard about this wagon and its contents—'

'Everybody's heard about it,' Bren cut in, 'because it's spread all over the newspapers.'

Gamboa waved his waved his cigar airily.

'But of that everybody, we will be the first to make a move. It has to be that way. So, I had heard that the Coogan brothers were men who would act without hesitation; without wasting time. Those brothers, I decided, are the men I need to help me steal the money.' He narrowed his eyes. 'But all men can become over confident, and make mistakes—'

'Especially those,' Mick Coogan said, 'who act without hesitation,' and he winked broadly at his brother.

The irony was lost on Gamboa.

'Indeed, especially those,' he said. 'So when looking ahead to tomorrow we must try to understand the way other men think, and when we have reached conclusions we must plan accordingly.'

'My conclusion is that an escort gives the game away, tells the world that something of great value is being transported,' Bren Coogan said.

'The game's already up,' Mick said, 'if the shipment of gold's been announced in the newspapers.'

'An armed escort would be like a finger pointing at the actual wagon, singling it out from all the other wagons on the trail. My armed escort would be two or three men with rifles, inside the wagon, under all that canvas.'

'Shotguns are great levellers,' his brother said, 'and we've got three of them.'

'And if that's not enough of a surprise,' said Bren, 'we'll be shooting at them out of the darkness. There'll be no logs laid across the road, no warning that would enable the wagon to slow down and give the men inside time to react. An ambush is the way it'll be done. We'll wipe them out before they have time to react.'

'Is that the way? Slaughter the lot of them?'

'Dead men don't tell tales, Mick. Besides, we need the wagon.'

'The wagon will be pulled by mules,' Gamboa said. 'There will be a driver, a man riding shotgun. If you are right, two or three men inside makes at least five, and we are outnumbered.'

'But only two out in the open, up on the boot,' Bren Coogan said.

'Sitting there like ducks,' Mick said.

Smoke trickled from Gamboa's flared nostrils. He was nodding slowly.

'I have recently ridden through the perfect place for this ambush. West of Gila Bend there is a settlement called Agua Caliente. It is on the north bank of the Gila. But on the south bank the trail between Yuma and Gila Bend twists and turns as it passes through woods. In that place we can arrange it so that the Conestoga wagon is caught between us.'

Bren Coogan nodded. 'One man positions himself in the woods so that he's able to watch the wagon approach. With a shotgun, he can cut down the two men up on the boot. If the others wait in the woods then come in behind the wagon, they'll be ideally placed to deal with the men I truly believe will be in there under the canvas.'

'They hear the gunfire they're bound to show themselves,' Mick said.

'The moment they do that,' Bren said, 'it will all be over.'

For several minutes the three men smoked in silence. Then Bren Coogan stood up. He walked a little way out of the trees, stood looking down at the river.

'How far is it to those woods at Agua Caliente, Gamboa?'

'From here, maybe twenty miles.'

'We set off now, spend the rest of the day in the woods setting up the ambush. That gives us all day tomorrow to rest up.'

'When it's done,' Mick Coogan said, 'are we heading back to La Buena Tierra?'

'Gamboa?' Bren said, swinging on the Mexican. 'You know this river. Can we take a loaded Conestoga wagon across here?'

'If the mules are willing, yes, for sure we can.'

'That's it then. When this is over and done I can't think of a place to hole up where there's less chance of anyone finding us.'

SIX

It was a sombre Frank Carson who walked into Lars Sorensen's office the next morning. A couple of deputies were there, finishing off their coffee and getting final instructions from the marshal. His eagle eye alighted on Carson and he at once spotted that there was something amiss. Gesturing to a chair, he quickly wrapped up the early morning meeting and the two deputies left to go about their various duties.

'Brand in trouble?' Sorensen said, sitting back and giving Carson his full attention.

'He died in the night,' Carson said, forcing the words out, still numb with shock. 'Never regained consciousness.'

'Dammit,' Sorensen said softly, and there was genuine pain in his eyes as he let the silence build.

'Doc Hall's arranging the burial for later today, but. . . .'

He let his voice trail off as, inexplicably, he lost the thread.

Sorensen said gently, 'Yeah, go on, but what?'

'It must be obvious I've got other things on my mind. If what you said last night is correct and those two ex-cons are going to make a try for that Conestoga wagon, I want to be there. Now, more than ever, I've got a score to settle.'

Sorensen frowned. 'I sympathize with you, fellow, but as a Texas Ranger you know that's not the way to go about it. I'd also point out that you'll be crossing swords with federal lawmen.'

'Don't jump to conclusions. I didn't specify what form that settling would take.'

'No, you left it to my imagination, and that's bad enough.' Sorensen grimaced. 'You might be interested to know I've already been up at the prison talking to the governor. He says neither Kade nor Hood took kindly to being locked up, but if there's going to be trouble it'll come from Hood. During his spell inside, Kade acted up out of frustration. According to the governor, Hood's bad through and through.'

For a few moments the two men sat without talking. After declining the offer of coffee, Carson had half-turned his chair and he was gazing absently through the office's open door. Yuma's main street was bustling. Wagons and horsemen were kicking up dust, and the shrill cries of mule-skinners and bull-whackers mingled with the thud of hoofs and the squeal of wagon wheels.

Watching them, listening to the noise, Carson said, 'What time's this Conestoga expected through here?'

'You think anybody's bothered to tell me? Take a wild guess. Could be any time between dawn and dusk. You ask me, the whole business is a farce.'

'But your deputies are watching for it?'

'Oh, they'll let me know if they spot it, then it's like you said yesterday: I see it through here, then wash my hands of it.'

'If it makes it this far.'

Sorensen raised an eyebrow, then smiled wickedly.

'Good point. Be helpful if it got waylaid on some dusty trail in California.'

'On the other hand,' Carson said, 'if it does make it this far it could be the perfect bait, the lure to catch the fish. Can't you see it? Kade and Hood are attracted to it like bears to a honey pot, I lie in wait, take them when they pounce.'

'To do that,' Sorensen said, 'you'd have to follow that Conestoga wagon. With Brand gone you're on your own—'

'I can handle it.'

'I'm sure you can. But if we're wrong about those ex-cons, if they're already a hundred miles away and heading Christ knows where, that wagon could bounce its way clear across Arizona without incident and you'd be in for a long and frustrating ride.'

Carson nodded, realizing Sorensen was right, understanding – as the sharp shock of Brand's death began to dull – that he was allowing a natural desire for revenge to divert him from the task he and Brand had set themselves. Two Texas Rangers bound in a common cause, they had ridden for many months and several hundred miles in pursuit of the elusive Lope Gamboa. That cause could not be abandoned, and there was no obvious link between Gamboa and the two ex-cons called Kade and Hood.

Did that rule out the Conestoga wagon as a way of getting at Gamboa?

No, it did not. There was a clear link between Gamboa and the Coogan brothers. Before Kade and Hood walked down the slope from the jail and committed murder, Sorensen and other shrewd brains sincerely believed Gamboa had joined the Coogans to form a hard-hitting team that would lift the Conestoga's cash. So, forget Kade and Hood. The Coogans would hit the Conestoga wagon. Riding with them would be the 'breed killer, Lope Gamboa.

Carson took a deep breath of pure relief, and at that moment the bright sunlight was blocked as a tall man appeared in the office doorway. As he stepped over the threshold, a feeling that could only be described as a terrible feeling of foreboding swept over Carson. He struggled to his feet, sensing – without knowing why – that the course of events was about to take a dramatic turn and that somehow it would be up to him to determine if that change would be for the better, or for the worse.

The tall man's glance swept over him. Then the newcomer turned to Sorensen.

'In most towns I've ever passed through, the place to go for information is the saloon, or that office occupied by the minions of the law,' he said. 'The saloon's closed. Do you know why?'

He was dressed in black. His voice was soft but deep, his grey eyes watchful, his movements cat-like. Broad shoulders tapered to a narrow waist. Strong hands hung relaxed, the right brushing a worn Colt .45.

'The owner was involved in an . . . accident.'

'Which leaves you: the lawman.'

Sorensen was also on his feet.

'This is beginning to sound ominous. Who are you, mister, and what is it you want?'

'It's not who I am, but who I'm after,' the tall newcomer said. 'I'd be very much obliged if either of you gents could point me in the direction of a greasy cut-throat by the name of Lope Gamboa.'

PART TWO

SEVEN

By midday, the saloonist's wife had arranged for her brother to stand in as barman, and the saloon was open for business. It was to that cool establishment that Frank Carson and the tall newcomer repaired in the heat of the day when Lars Sorensen, with obvious relief, was called away by one of his deputies.

Over a cold glass of beer taken at a table well away from the crowded bar, Carson studied the tall stranger.

'A greasy cut-throat. Described that way, I'd say Gamboa is no friend of yours.'

'He's a complete stranger.'

'But you're looking for him?'

'Oh yes.'

'So tell me. His rich uncle's died, he's inherited the hacienda? His sister is with child, she wants him there for the birth?'

The tall man grinned. 'Could be all of those, and more. But even so, nothing changes.'

'You probably noticed I said very little back there in Sorensen's office. I'll say it now. I was intrigued because you strode in out of nowhere and mentioned the name Gamboa. I'm a Texas Ranger. I've been hunting that man for a long time.'

'Really?' Mention of the Texas Rangers had suddenly aroused the tall man's interest. For a moment he stared hard at Carson, his eyes unreadable. Then he said, 'Any luck?'

'None. Until yesterday.'

'Ah.' The tall man nodded. 'That means you've heard something, you've not yet acted on the information, and you're not going to share your knowledge until you know more about me.'

'That's about it.'

'I've got nothing to hide. My name's Joe Creed. Until a couple of years ago I was a deputy marshal down in Laredo. One day I was drinking in a cantina, over the Bravo in Nuevo Laredo. An old Mex' bandit came up with the name Gamboa. He was telling a bloody story to a couple of cronies, shooting, killing, rape and pillage – that kind of stuff. Suddenly what he was talking about began to make sense because he got down to particulars such as dates and places and it all became too damn familiar for comfort. I went back across the river and handed in my badge and from that day to this I've been . . . put bluntly, I've been chasing a shadow, a ghost.' He shrugged. 'What about you? Why are the rangers after Gamboa?'

'He cut one throat too many. A Texas Ranger died. Before that he'd committed atrocities across the West, sometimes with Indians, sometimes with white renegades.'

Creed nodded, his eyes suddenly narrow with speculation and something that, to Carson, looked very much like the kindling of hope.

'That explains your motives,' Creed said, as if mentally shaking himself, 'but what about my tale? Have I told you enough to be taken into your confidence?'

'Well, your story rings true, and I'm in need of support. My partner died suddenly. If I really am getting close to Gamboa, a sidekick would improve my chances when I run him down. You're an ex-lawman, and you look . . . capable.'

Creed ducked his head in acknowledgement.

'So what have you heard that suggests you're nearing the end of a long hunt?'

Carson settled back and began talking. After five minutes and another glass of beer, Creed knew all about the Conestoga wagon carrying government money, the Coogans, and the ex-cons Kade and Hood. Carson told him all he had learnt from Sorensen, but emphasized that there was a lot of speculation; that the only certainty was that Deakin Hood had murdered Texas Ranger Eddie Brand and that – no more than a reasonable expectation – sometime that day the Conestoga wagon would pass through Yuma on the start of its journey across Arizona.

'Nevertheless,' Creed said, when Carson had finished, 'speculation becomes damn close to a certainty if, like me, you've spent years looking into the workings of the criminal mind. Then there's that fellow down the street, Sorensen, he's town marshal and so we've got three lawmen coming to the same conclusion and asking the same question: there are known criminal elements in the area; rich pickings are about to fall into their laps; what are they going to do?'

'They'll go after that cash, for certain,' Carson said. 'As you say, that's easy. But when we look closer, things get messy. We know of two separate bands of desperadoes. There could be others, but let's keep it reasonably simple. If they hit the Conestoga at different locations, one band gets lucky, the other rides away empty handed. Could be doubly tough on the driver and his shotgun, but that doesn't concern us – and it's of no concern to Sorensen if it happens outside the town limits.'

'Brings us back to Gamboa, doesn't it?' Creed says. 'Gamboa's with those Irish fellows, the Coogans. The Coogan band is one of two we're pretty damned certain is going to hit a government Conestoga wagon loaded with cash. So if we want Gamboa—'

'We've got to be close to the wagon when it's hit.' Carson nodded. 'I already mentioned that to Sorensen. He said if I've got it wrong I'm in for a long and ultimately wasted ride.'

'Did he suggest an alternative?'

'Creed, there is no alternative,' Carson said.

Creed nodded. He downed his beer, then scraped back his chair and stood up.

'Let's go see if there's any news.'

They walked out into the dazzling early afternoon sunshine and for a few moments stood there accustoming themselves once again to the light and heat and the noise and dust of the busy town.

Carson was impressed with the tall Creed's demeanour and decisiveness, and immensely relieved that the big man had ridden into Yuma to stand in for the irreplaceable Eddie Brand in the hunt for Lope Gamboa. But in what he hoped were the final stages of that long and exhausting hunt there were too many imponderables for Carson's liking. Rumour and speculation put Gamboa with the Coogans, just as that same rumour had the Coogans hitting the Conestoga wagon. But if the newspaper reports were wrong and the wagon failed to pass through Yuma—'

'Well, lookee down there,' Creed said in his deep, gentle tones. 'Damn me if a deputy isn't haring up the street towards the jail and he's only just outpacing what looks awful like that wagon we've been discussing.'

'With a cavalry escort,' Carson said, squinting into the sunlight.

He strode towards the edge of the plank walk. Away down the street the deputy had reached the jail. He stood outside, shouting. Sorensen burst through the door, slapping his hat on his head while clinging to his unbuckled gun-belt. As marshal and deputy watched, then ran to their horses, the Conestoga wagon trundled past, six stiff-eared mules kicking up clouds of dust. The dust drifted back over the driver with his snaking whip, the shotgun guard sitting gripping the box, the white canvas that billowed behind them and the four blue-clad United States cavalrymen who rode two to either side of jolting, creaking vehicle.

Passers by paused to watch. Behind Carson and

Creed, men came pouring from the saloon, threatening to push them into the street. Inexorably, oblivious to what was going on all around, driver and escort brought the wagon up the street. It rocked past the saloon, the snorting of the mules and the creek and thunder of its passing assailing the senses. In its wake rode Lars Sorensen and his deputy.

Sorensen turned his head and saw Carson. The two men's eyes met. Carson thought he saw Sorensen raise an eyebrow, as if asking a silent question.

Then he turned away, dust drifted across the plank walk to drive the onlookers back into the saloon, and the little cavalcade had passed.

'Where's your horse?' Carson said.

'In the barn, same as yours.'

Carson stepped down into the dust and led the way across the street.

'There's no hurry,' he said. 'It's not going to get away from us, and at least a couple of things have been settled: there's a wagon; it's got an escort.'

'Trouble is that's good news and bad news,' Creed said. 'I'd've been a damn sight happier with no escort. Supposing the Coogans'll hide in the scrub, take one look at those horse soldiers and give it up as a bad job? They do that, Gamboa's as far away as ever.'

'I've just about had my fill of speculation,' Carson said as they reached the livery barn and paused outside the double doors. 'Maybe they will, maybe they won't. Every time I turn around there's a question mark hanging in the air.'

Creed was grinning.

'That's just me thinking aloud. But thinking never did hold me back, nor even slow me down.'

So saying the tall man turned on his heel and strode into the barn.

Although Carson had stressed that there was no need to hurry, they wasted no time in saddling their horses. Within minutes they were back on the street. Moving economically they threaded their way through the seething mêlée of horses and wagons and so made their way up the street. When the buildings began to thin on either side and they reached the outskirts of town, the lie of the land was such that no Conestoga wagon was visible: the trail east meandered through stands of parched trees and barren hillocks before flattening into the monotonous desert terrain that was typical of that part of the West; the land beyond their immediate location, stretching into the vast distances, was lost to view.

Sorensen and his deputy were, at that moment, riding around one of those arid knolls on their way back to town. As they drew near Carson saw at once that, instead of looking relieved at seeing off the Conestoga wagon, Sorensen's face wore a puzzled frown.

'That newspaper journalist got the wagon right, and he got the date right,' he said, drawing rein alongside Carson and Creed. 'As for the rest, one thing is clearly wrong, which puts much that came after those details into doubt.'

'You questioned those troopers, and there is no cash?' Carson said.

'Didn't get close enough, didn't intend to. But what I saw with my own eyes told me something's wrong. That wagon is not following the old Oxbow route. A half-mile out of town, 'stead of pushing steadily on that north east line, it veered sharply away to the south. If it keeps on that heading it'll finish up on the Mex' border, every mile taking it further and further away from where the Coogans and those two ex-cons are likely lying in wait.

EIGHT

Once Carson and Creed were through the encircling region of mostly insignificant bluffs and knolls that yet caused the trail out of Yuma to wind this way and that, the Conestoga wagon with its flapping canvas and escort of cavalrymen was clearly visible – albeit as a shimmering shape that in the heat-haze seemed to float several feet above the surface of a desert that from time to time appeared as a dark lake.

As they trailed the wagon on its journey that would eventually take it to the Mexican border and beyond, neither man seemed inclined to speak. Each was immersed in his own thoughts, and for Carson that meant he was desperately trying to make sense out of what was happening – and consequently of what he was doing.

Sorensen had warned him more than once that if he, Carson, followed the wagon he could be looking at an frustrating ride and a lot of wasted time: if neither outlaw faction tried to seize the cash – or if the hold-up was staged by Kade and Hood – his search for Lope Gamboa could be set back by days, perhaps months.

But now the marshal's warning seemed doubly ominous because the Conestoga wagon didn't seem to be following the rules laid down by the journalist who'd broken the story. As Sorensen so rightly pointed out, if the journalist had got one thing wrong then the whole story printed in the newspaper was standing on shaky foundations. But where lay the truth? Had an ambitious journalist with a newfangled typewriter let rip with his imagination? Or had he been fed a story by someone setting out deliberately to mislead?

The only flimsy justification Carson would allow himself for his dogged tracking of the wagon was that if the outlaw factions had an ounce of brain between them they wouldn't have relied solely on the newspaper reports. Like anyone else, they would have read the report with a huge chunk of scepticism, and common sense said they would have put someone close to Yuma to watch events unfold. If they'd done that, they'd at once have spotted the wagon's altered route.

Which meant, Carson told himself, that they were out there somewhere just waiting for the right time to attack.

The trouble was, as Creed pointed out when Carson broke the long silence and made that point to him late that afternoon, in that flat, barren landscape of sun-scorched dust and sand there was nowhere for anybody to hide. If outlaws were out there, Creed said, they'd be seen. If they couldn't be seen. . . .

'They're not there,' Carson said glumly.

'They're not,' Creed said, 'but sure as hell someone is – and to me they look awful like a couple of those cavalry troopers.'

He gestured with his thumb. Carson twisted in the saddle to look over his shoulder. Two blue-clad mounted figures were closing fast. Both riders were carrying rifles.

'We've been riding in our sleep,' Carson said bitterly. 'If we'd been watching with half an eye we'd've seen them slip away from the wagon. Hell, you've just told me there's nowhere out here for a man to hide, yet they've managed to sneak up on us.'

'Had a feeling something like this might happen,' Creed said philosophically. 'You start tailing the military you're asking for trouble.'

'So we keep our hands in sight, and smile,' Carson said.

There was no expression on the faces of the two men who caught up with them then split apart to take up position on either side of Carson and Creed. One was dark, one fair, both dusty and streaked with sweat.

'May I ask what you two men are up to?'

The swarthy cavalryman with two chevrons of rank on his sleeve spoke directly to Carson. His rifle rested almost casually across his thighs, but his finger was on the trigger.

'We have reason to believe the load that wagon's carrying is an open invitation to outlaws,' Carson said, picking his words. 'We know of two groups in the area:

the Coogan brothers, and a couple of cons fresh out of Yuma jail.'

'And?'

'We believe you'll be attacked. My guess is it'll happen at dusk, or soon after.'

The cavalryman who'd taken up the left flank was grinning. The corporal raised an eyebrow.

'We're an armed escort, feller. Don't you think the possibility of ambush might have occurred to us?'

'It's always handy,' Carson said, 'to have experienced back up when things go wrong.'

The swarthy corporal's eyes narrowed.

'Are you saying we're not up to the job?'

'No—'

'And what do you mean by experienced?'

Carson dipped two fingers into his vest pocket and pulled out the badge of the Texas Ranger: a glittering star within a silver circle.

The corporal rolled his eyes, then looked across at Creed.

'What about you?'

Creed grinned. 'I'm with him.'

'Jesus!'

Turning his head aside and spitting in disgust the corporal said, 'Come on, you're riding down with us, there's a man wants to talk to you.'

Half a mile ahead, the wagon had pulled up alongside just about the only stand of trees within ten square miles. Carson and Creed rode ahead of the two cavalrymen. As they drew closer to the wagon party they saw that the driver and his shotgun, middle-aged men with straggling moustaches and long hair, had come down from the box and were sitting with their backs against the big wheels. A third cavalryman, a big fellow with sergeant's chevrons on his sleeve, was drinking from a water bottle. He came forward to meet them.

'Texas Rangers,' the corporal said, swinging out of the saddle. 'They're here to save us from outlaws out there waiting to ambush us.'

The big sergeant poked a finger inside his shirt and scratched his hairy chest.

'Much appreciated,' he said with heavy sarcasm. 'Tell me, what are these outlaws after?'

'The cash you're carrying,' Carson said.

Deadpan, the sergeant thrust a hand into his pants pocket and brought out a ten-cent piece. He held it up. It shone in the facing light.

'You mean this?'

'I mean the government cash you're carrying in that wagon.'

There was a moment's silence. Then the sergeant crooked a finger. He led the way to the rear of the wagon, swept the canvas to one side with a big fist and invited Carson to step closer.

'You see any cash in there?'

The sergeant was standing close to Carson. His breath reeked of alcohol. Carson poked his head inside the wagon. He saw stacks of oblong boxes. Printing was stencilled on the sides. In the oppressive heat trapped under the canvas there was the smell of machine oil.

Carson stepped back.

'I see boxes purporting to contain rifles and

ammunition. That doesn't mean they do.'

The sergeant nodded slowly.

'Oh, yes, that's what's in there, I can assure you of that. If I'm wrong, a certain officer over there at Fort Huachuca in eastern Arizona is surely going to blow his top.'

'Then if you are right you won't mind me taking a look. Opening one of those boxes?'

Something ugly stirred in the sergeant's eyes.

'Are you saying I'm lying?'

'No. But it's possible someone in authority is using you—'

'And *that's* as good as calling me a fool.' The sergeant's grin was a challenge. 'So which is it, feller? Am I a liar, or a fool?'

'Any box,' Carson said doggedly. 'I choose one at random. You open it. If it's packed with rifles, then I'm the fool, not you.'

For a moment the sergeant stood there, big fists clenched, and it could have swung either way. Then he gestured to the swarthy corporal.

'Climb up there. He points, you open.'

Again the canvas was swept to one side. The corporal swung a leg up and climbed into the wagon. He bent, looked back.

Carson pointed. 'That one. Next to the end.'

There was a short iron pinch bar on the wagon's floor. The corporal used it to prise up the box's lid. The nails resisted with squeals that put a man's teeth on edge, then gave suddenly and the lid popped up.

'Get in there,' the sergeant growled.

Knowing he truly was making a fool of himself, Carson climbed into the wagon. The corporal was holding the lid open. Carson looked in at the rows of rifles packed in grease, and felt his jaw tighten. He nodded, climbed back down and faced the sergeant.

Carson bit his lip. He looked at Creed, who was standing well back out of the way. Then, as the corporal began noisily hammering down the lid, he shook his head.

'We know a Conestoga wagon was due to come through Yuma today, carrying government money—'

'How do you know?'

'It's no secret. Everybody in Yuma knows. It was in the newspaper—'

'And you believed that?'

Carson took a deep breath.

'The story must have been checked by the editor. No editor would print an unsubstantiated story—'

'My education doesn't stretch to knowing what that means but I'm telling you, feller, there is no wagon carrying cash. There is no cash. I give as much credence to items I read in newspapers as I'd give to an Injun telling me he doesn't touch whiskey. If a piece in a newspaper is supposed to be reporting something said by one of them politicians – I treat it like the bullshit it assuredly is. The newspaper's wrong: there's no cash; there's no wagon.'

Looking at him, looking at the earnest face burned by the sun and meeting those honest blue eyes set in crinkled flesh, Carson was almost inclined to believe him. But the honest blue eyes were bloodshot, and

Carson couldn't forget that on the big man's breath there was a strong smell of whiskey.

So it was almost – but not quite.

NINE

The oil lamps were lit when they rode wearily into Yuma. Creed pulled his horse away from Frank Carson as they drew level with the saloon.

'After that farce out there I can almost taste that beer, feel the cool liquid trickling down my throat,' he said. 'You go talk to Sorensen. Shouldn't take you too long to tell him we got nowhere. There'll be a full glass waiting on the bar when you're through.'

'Don't get too settled,' Carson said as the tall man swung down and began tying up at the hitch rail. 'Something tells me this night's not over by a long shot.'

He pushed on down the almost deserted street. As usual there was a light shining in Sorensen's office and, when Carson pushed open the door, he saw that it was the marshal himself keeping a lonely vigil from behind his littered desk. The look he gave Carson when he walked in told the ranger that his troubles were nowhere near over. He flipped his hat at one of the wooden hooks, saw it spin wide, hit the wall and flop to the floor, and shrugged.

'That about sums up most of my day,' he said, slumping into a chair. 'Though I guess anything would be an improvement on what Eddie Brand's been through.' He looked glumly at Sorensen. 'Did my partner's burial go OK?'

'He's been planted,' Sorensen said. 'Crude way to put it, but there's nothing refined about a six by three patch of earth on boot hill.' He shrugged. 'If your day was bad I don't need to ask if you were chasin' the right wagon.'

'Depends on who it was supposed to be right for. It was right for the troops garrisoned at Fort Huachuca, because they're short of weapons and that Conestoga was carrying all they need. But right for me, right for those owlhoots? Definitely not. About the only cash anywhere near it was a ten cent piece sitting in a sergeant's pocket.'

'Actually,' Sorensen said, 'I was making a statement, not asking a question. I don't need to ask if that was the right wagon because I know damn well it wasn't. The right wagon went through Yuma an hour after I got back to town. Came over the crossing, rattled up main street, went on through and took the turn that newspaper said it would. By now it'll be pushing on along the Oxbow route, the driver and his mate maybe looking for a place to bed down for the night.'

'Damn it,' Carson said softly. 'So the newspaper was right, but it forgot to point out there could be more than one Conestoga.'

'We all should have known that, probably did know

72

but chose to ignore the obvious. Me because I couldn't wait to see the back of it, see it clear of my town. You because you've got this Lope Gamboa on your mind and that obsession's making you blind to everything else.'

'Not so blind that I couldn't see the cavalry sergeant was lying through his teeth. Not so blind that I can't see you're holding something back, Sorensen.'

'How did he lie?'

'Told me point blank there was no wagon, no cash.'

'What makes that a lie?'

'The look on his face made it a lie. And now the look on your face is telling me you know something that just about proves he was lying.'

Sorensen sighed, then yawned and kicked his long legs up onto the desk.

'I don't know any such thing, Carson,' he said, pulling a face, 'but I'm beginning to believe there's something mighty queer going on.' He frowned, rocked gently in his chair and said, 'When you caught up with that wagon, what did you notice about the driver and fellow riding shotgun?'

'Notice?'

'Were they old, young, middling?'

'Not young. Forties or fifties. Grizzled old-timers is how I'd describe them. Why?'

'Is that different, or the same as most wagon drivers you've come across over the years?'

'I've never yet seen a wagon driver of any kind that didn't come out of that very same mould.'

'Me neither. Which is why I thought it odd that the

73

two fellows sitting up on the box of that second Conestoga that drove through were young. I'd put them in their twenties – but only just.'

'Leading to what conclusion, exactly?'

'Those grizzled old-timers you described have one thing in common: their heads are packed with the wisdom that comes from experience. My conclusion is this: that wagon driver and his shotgun buddy were young because whoever's behind this business couldn't find any wise old-timers foolish enough to take on the job.'

'Why?'

'Because they know they'd be committing suicide.'

Carson sat back, thinking hard. Sorensen tossed the makings onto the desk. They slid towards Carson. He shook his head.

'Creed's got a drink waiting for me, but after that long and frustrating ride I wouldn't say no to coffee.'

While the marshal clattered pots and cups at the stove, Carson mulled over what had been said. Inevitably he found himself going back over *everything* that had been said in the past couple of days, and he knew that the conclusion Sorensen had reached had been staring them in the face.

'Only reason that piece was put in the newspaper was to draw attention to the wagon,' he said. 'Only possible reason anyone could want attention drawn to a wagonload of cash is because it's a decoy. And if it is a decoy, that reporter didn't come up with a story, he was ordered to write it by someone much higher up.'

'And the only way it could be a decoy without being

a mighty expensive one,' Sorensen said, placing two steaming cups on the desk, 'is if the money doesn't exist.'

'Or it exists, but somewhere a long way from that Conestoga wagon. The first time we talked, I said it'd be safer moved by rail. You think that's what's going on? The wagon draws the outlaws, while they're occupied the money slips through unnoticed?'

'No, that possibility's been ruled out.' Sorensen used a finger to flick a slip of paper lying on his desk. 'This wire came in late this afternoon. There's been a dry landslip over the border in California. A good section of the Southern Pacific's track has been wiped out, could be as much as half a mile. Trains won't be running for a week or more.'

Carson frowned. 'But news of the wagon and its load has already been in the newspaper. If the landslip is the reason for moving that cash by road, it must have occurred days ago.'

'Likely it did. Doesn't change anything.'

'In a way it does. Suddenly we can see why a wagon's being used: with the Southern Pacific out of action in these parts it was the only option, and they're in a hurry. The way I see it now, the wagon's taking the Oxbow route with the idea of linking up with the Atchison, Topeka.'

Sorensen stared broodingly into his mug.

'This business of a decoy seems an awful complicated way of going about things,' he said. 'Easy way of ensuring the cash stays safe would be to keep everything secret from the start.'

'Which would rule out a calculated attempt to create a decoy, and put us back with a reporter leaking the story,' Carson said. He grimaced. 'So . . . what is going on? You say it's complicated, but maybe it's a damn sight more complicated than it looks.'

'I'm getting dizzy trying to work it out,' Sorensen said, 'and I've already made it clear I'm done with that wagon now it's left Yuma. But what about you? Have you figured out your next move?'

'How much start has that second wagon got?'

Sorensen glanced across at the big wall clock.

'At least four hours.'

'Then if we're going to catch Gamboa, me and Creed had better get moving.'

'Unfortunately, there's a lot of ifs that could pile up to spoil your night,' Sorensen said. 'For instance, you stand no chance of catching Gamboa if he's not out there. And if he is out there, you can only catch him if you get there before he and those Coogans hit the wagon.' He watched impassively as Carson rose to leave. 'And staying with that two-letter word, if you want my opinion you're already way too late.'

TEN

Kade and Hood picked up the Conestoga wagon as it came rattling and squeaking out of Yuma and pulled a long trail of dust onto the Oxbow route. They were sitting on the old ranch wagon's box, back in the trees and hidden from sight in a small hollow but with a clear view of the town and its approaches. They had been there most of the afternoon. This was the second wagon they had spotted.

'That first Conestoga has me worried,' Kade said. 'I tell you, I still can't be sure we've got it right.'

'Meaning you can't be sure *I've* got it right,' Hood said. Then he chuckled. 'Maybe I've got a better idea of the way a politician's mind works. You saw that wagon's military escort. Providing a wagon with an escort like that is as good as telling the world there's something valuable on board. Why do that? I'll tell you why. Because that's exactly what those politicians hope every damn bandit in the area will believe – they'll believe it, and maybe they'll try an ambush and maybe they won't, but whatever they do or don't do they're guaranteed to wind up empty-handed.'

'Meanwhile,' Kade said softly, 'the wagon that's carrying the cash slips through unnoticed.'

'You got it.'

Kade stared off, narrow eyed. He was watching the dust settling behind the lumbering Conestoga wagon which was already more than half a mile away. What Hood said made some sense, but also posed questions. For instance, according to the route announced in the paper, that first wagon with its escort had gone the wrong way.

Then again, maybe that was another example of crafty thinking. The first Conestoga wagon had headed south. The escort suggested there was a valuable cargo. That attracted the bandits, and they were led further and further in the wrong direction.'

'You see it?' Hood said, watching him.

'Sure. You're making a lot of sense. So now we do what we said we'd do: we go after that wagon, we overtake it and pick our spot.'

'Be dusk by the time we've done that,' Hood said. 'It'll be easy pickings.'

They caught the Conestoga wagon after a three-mile chase and went clattering past with two wheels off the trail and the Conestoga's sweating driver and his shotgun hanging on grimly as they cast disbelieving glances at the farm-wagon's strange rig.

'Tongue snapped clear in two,' Hood yelled, as the two wagons rocked axle to axle. 'Injured two horses, left us with this.'

He gestured ahead to where the two saddled broncs with stirrups tied were reluctantly playing the part of team mules, and rolled his eyes in mock disgust.

Then they bounced back onto the trail and with Kade standing and making a grand show of flicking the makeshift traces they rapidly left the Conestoga wallowing in their dusty wake.

They pushed on hard. When the light began to fail Hood estimated the Conestoga was a mile behind them. When dusk was upon them that distance had increased to two miles and, when dark timber closed in on the narrowing trail creating impenetrable walls of vegetation on either side, he called a halt.

'We swing this wagon across the trail about here,' he said, 'there's no way they can get past.'

They unhitched the two horses and tethered them back in the trees. Then, puffing and grunting, they used their shoulders to work the farm wagon backwards and forwards until it was broadside on and the trail was blocked.

Kade stepped back. Hands on hips he looked at what they'd done, and shook his head.

'It was a good idea of yours, Hood, but when that's loaded we'll never move it. If we want to get to that ranch, La Buena Tierra, we need to turn this thing so it's facing back down the trail.'

Hood mopped his brow, glared at Kade and cursed softly. Again they set to. Ten minutes later, their backs aching, the wagon was back with all four wheels on the trail and the broken tongue pointing towards the west.

'Satisfied?'

'Getting there. Once the cargo's been switched, the Conestoga'll have to be moved out of the way – but we'll worry about that when the time comes. Let's take the horses back down the trail a ways. Far enough so that when that Conestoga's forced to halt, we can mount up and come in behind them.'

'That was my idea too,' Hood said. 'You happy with it?'

Kade pursed his lips and frowned.

'Now you ask, no, I'm not. We should split up. You go back down the trail, I'll push on fifty yards. That way they'll be caught in the middle. Soon as that wagon stops, we make our move.'

'Sounds like you're taking over, big man.'

'Just offering my advice,' Kade said. 'And here's the best bit – which I know I'm repeating but what the hell – if it can be worked, we do this without shooting, without a drop of blood being shed.'

A faint moon was visible above the tops of the tall pines when Kade caught the first faint sounds announcing the approach of the Conestoga. He was sprawled on his back on a bed of needles, hands behind his head, looking up at the gently swaying branches just visible against the darkening skies as he reflected with considerable seriousness on his change of circumstances. A couple of days ago a prisoner, now a free man – but contemplating committing an act that would get him sent back inside for a long time if he was caught. If that wasn't enough, he couldn't help recalling the broad wink Hood had given him and reminding himself that the man could not be trusted. They were in this together out of necessity. Once the job was done, Kade knew damn well he'd have to watch his back.

Faintly he heard the cry of the Conestoga's driver. Still moving, wanting to cover as much distance as he could while there was still light to see a hand in front of him. And why not? If he had that much cash sitting behind him, Kade figured, and the knowledge that there were thieves out there waiting to pounce, he'd want to drive forever, keep moving, get to wherever the hell he was going as fast as possible.

A horse whinnied. More sounds, closer, the crackle of twigs, the snapping of a branch, and Kade knew Hood was preparing to move. Reluctantly, Kade climbed to his feet, slapped on his hat. The Texas Ranger's horse turned to nuzzle him as he moved close. He patted its warm neck, then swung into the saddle and moved to the edge of the trees. There was still enough light to see down the trail. Looking across the top of the old ranch wagon, he saw a flash of white as Hood waved a hand. He returned the signal, loosened the six-gun in its holster, took a deep, deep breath.

The Conestoga was on them abruptly, appearing as a billowing white shape rounding a kink in the trail and pushing on looking bulky and unstoppable. But the ranch wagon was there, blocking the way forward. Suddenly the driver was up on his feet and hauling on the traces. Snorting, the mules dug in, eyes rolling white as the weight of the Conestoga threatened to run them down.

The shotgun guard was also up. He was bracing

himself as the wagon shuddered to a halt, holding the shotgun at the port as he swung this way and that, peering into the gathering gloom.

Looking back, he spotted movement. He shouted a warning, swung the shotgun. As it came around, from back down the trail there was a crack and a bright muzzle flash. The guard roared in pain. The shotgun flew from his hands. He sat down, clutching his shoulder.

Adam Kade kneed his horse out onto the trail.

Six-gun out and cocked, he called, 'Hold it there. No more sudden moves. Just relax and nobody'll get hurt.'

'Bit late for that,' the driver said, and he turned and spat. 'What the hell is this?'

'A hold-up,' Deakin Hood said.

He'd ridden up behind the Conestoga. Now he brought his horse around it, waggling his six-gun at the driver.

'You two boys can make a choice. Help us move your load to that wagon there, or we do it ourselves after making damn sure you're no danger to us.'

The guard, his face pinched and white, shook his head.

'What the hell do you want with our load? You got a big family to feed?'

'If we have,' Hood said, 'that gold you're carrying will be a big help. So what's it to be?'

'Thanks to you, my partner's in no fit state—'

'It's you I'm talking to. I want that load shifted, and fast. So what's it to be, dead hero, or the driver who fought gallantly and lived to tell the tale?'

ELEVEN

In the woods on the south bank of the Gila River, a short way west of Agua Caliente, two Irishmen and a half-breed were waiting. They waited in the Stygian darkness of night and with a measure of unease, for some misgivings had been voiced.

Brendan Coogan had cursed softly but with colourful imagination because they had not factored into their plans the possibility that the Conestoga wagon loaded with government gold would stop and pull off the trail as soon as the light began to fail.

The 'breed, Lope Gamboa, had openly expressed his disgust, suggesting that perhaps his decision to work with the Coogan brothers had been a very big mistake.

Mick Coogan had cut short their poisonous bickering.

'If the wagon comes, it comes,' he said. 'If it doesn't, it'll come tomorrow and we do the job in daylight. What we do now is wait for a reasonable length of time. When it's obvious we've got it wrong, we bed down for the night.'

And so they waited. They waited while all around

83

them the night closed in and the silence that settled like a dark blanket was broken only by the haunting cries of nocturnal hunting creatures. They waited while high above the thin clouds a pale moon floated, dew settled coldly on leaves undisturbed by any breeze, and eyes ached from staring into distances where darkness was a barrier and nothing moved.

When they had waited in painful silence for more than an hour, the first sounds reached them.

'Dammit, we got it right,' Bren Coogan enthused.

'So now we take up our positions,' Lope Gamboa said practically. 'As I have the shotgun it will be my pleasure to cut down the driver and his guard when they approach. While that is happening, as those men die, the famous Coogan brothers who act without hesitation will be moving in from the rear to deal with the armed escort.'

'Would you listen to him?' Mick Coogan marvelled. 'He's been with us less than a week and he's taken over the whole damn show.'

'But I am right in what I say?'

'Oh, you're right, but all you're doing is echoing Brendan's words. You're a fake, Gamboa—'

'Enough,' Bren Coogan said. 'It's been said twice now, and it should be perfectly clear to all. Gamboa remains here with his shotgun and does what he has to do. We'll come in from behind, and if there is an escort hiding under that canvas and they emerge when we're upon them, then may God help them.'

They had tethered their horses deep in the woods. Mick and Bren Coogan slipped away. They moved down

84

the trail tight up against the trees in the shadows cast by the pale moon. At their sides there was the gleam of cold steel. Gamboa moved just a few yards. He chose a tree that gave him a clear view, and against that he leaned casually. The shotgun was held loosely in one hand. In the darkness his black eyes shone with an unholy light. The scar that distorted his mouth revealed glistening white teeth. Beneath the drooping moustache they were the teeth of a cruel predator.

The Conestoga's approach was slow. Its creaking and rattling and the jingle of harness were suggestive of an advancing army. As it drew nearer, as the eerie sounds increased, Gamboa's eyes grew smoky with an evil anticipation. His grip on the shotgun tightened. He lifted it, touched the blued barrels to his twisted lips. Then he settled the deadly weapon at an angle that would make a sudden spring into action smooth and unrestricted.

Like a ghost, the wagon approached. A hundred yards. Then fifty. Then twenty – and Gamboa lifted the shotgun to his shoulder, pressed his cheek to the cool wooden stock.

The Conestoga rocked on the rutted trail. Vapour rose from the hard-working mules, from their nostrils and from their glistening flanks. Gamboa could hear their snorts. Across the shotgun's levelled barrels and bead sight he could see their eyes shining and, above them, on the box, two men. One was slumped. The other held the traces lightly. Every now and then he called softly to the team.

Almost arrogantly, Lope Gamboa stepped out onto

the trail and took aim. He squeezed one trigger, rocked to the recoil, shifted aim and fired a second time.

The double explosion shattered the stillness of the night. Both men were caught by the dazzling muzzle flashes. Even though the bright flare lasted but a fraction of a second it was possible to see their terrible wounds. On faces, on bodies, blood glistened wetly. Then the light was gone. In its aftermath, the darkness was intense.

As the shotgun blasted and hot lead tore into timber, canvas and flesh, the mules panicked. Suddenly they were a tangled mass, rearing, squealing, caught by the harness, unable to flee. In their wild attempts to flee they pulled the wagon half off the trail and almost into the trees. It listed badly as the nearside wheels mounted a bank. Then one of the mules went down, kicking. The others were dragged to halt by the weight of the wagon, and the downed animal. They stood still, shivering, the whites of their rolling eyes the first thing Gamboa saw with any clarity as his vision cleared.

He stepped forward, licking his lips.

The driver and shotgun guard were down. As far as Gamboa could tell, the guard was dead, the driver alive but mortally wounded.

Then boots thudded on the trail. The Coogans came up behind the Conestoga. Brendan hung back. His pistol cracked as he fired twice, sending two bullets ripping high through the canvas. Ahead of him, Mick tore open the Conestoga's canvas. He ducked to one side. Waited, pistol held high. Then, carefully, he straightened up and looked inside.

'Nothing,' he cried. 'There's no escort. The damn wagon's ours.'

'What about the money, the gold?' Gamboa called.

'Wait.'

Mick climbed into the wagon. Both men, Gamboa and Brendan, could hear him banging about inside, the scrape of heavy objects being dragged. Less than half a minute later, he was out. His eyes were blazing as he looked at Brendan.

'There's nothing,' Mick said. 'They're carrying sacks of grain. Some of it's split open and spilled – but that's it.'

'We will see,' Gamboa said.

He let his shotgun fall. Then he drew the knife from its beaded sheath and climbed up onto the box. He looked at the guard. The man was young. He had fallen in a folded position. The boards beneath him were soaked with blood. Using his foot, Gamboa pushed him away. The body hit the trail with a thud. One hand flopped in the dust.

Gamboa turned to the driver – another young man. He had slumped back in his seat. The front of his shirt was peppered with holes, the material blood-soaked. His eyes glazing, his breathing moist and shallow. With a mighty effort he watched Gamboa and tried to rear backwards as the 'breed lifted the big knife and placed the point beneath the driver's chin.

The wagon rocked as Mick and Brendan climbed up. They hung on, watching.

'So now you tell us,' Gamboa said pleasantly. 'You tell us about the gold, and where it is.'

'Jesus,' the driver said hoarsely, 'not you too.'

Gamboa flicked a glance at Mick Coogan.

'Keep talking,' he said.

To force the driver's compliance, he began to put some pressure on the knife. Then, as a glistening drop of blood appeared on the driver's throat, he took the knife away. But not to remove it entirely. Instead, he lifted the blade higher, twisting it so that it reflected the faint light. As it moved up, across that grey face, the driver closed his eyes. Gamboa, eyes shining, placed the point of the knife against the driver's forehead. Swiftly, using the lightest of pressure, he drew the point of the razor-sharp blade down and across. Beneath it, skin that was stretched tightly across the bony skull was cleanly sliced open. As the point of the knife moved, so a beaded line of blood followed it. When Gamboa removed the blade, lifted it clear to survey his handiwork, the letter L was clearly visible. But that clarity was temporary. The letter, the initial letter of Gamboa's first name, rapidly blurred as blood seeped from the two cuts and spread across the driver's pale skin.

'Son of a bitch,' the driver croaked. 'All right, I'll tell you where it is, and a fat lot of good it'll do you. It's gone, that's where.'

'Gone where?' Gamboa snapped. 'Quickly, or I will finish you in a way you cannot imagine. This gold you were carrying is where?'

'Taken, that's where.'

Mick leaned forward, grasped his arm.

'Who took it?'

'It was taken by two men. They had a wagon. They stopped us, forced us to move the money. Then they drove off.'

'Drove where?' said Mick Coogan.

But he was too late. The driver was dead.

TWELVE

By the time Carson and Creed moved out of Yuma the moon was high, the thin cloud had cleared and it was an easy matter to pick up the sign left by the Conestoga wagon. The fresh ruts overlaid others left by wagons – few in number – that had earlier set out along the Oxbow route. With the signs as clear as a carefully drawn map the two men hunting Lope Gamboa were able to settle down to tracking the wagon with a minimum of effort.

Nevertheless, as the faint lights of Yuma fell behind them Carson was quick to voice his frustration.

'No matter how fast we go,' he said, 'time's against us. Consider it: how long did Sorensen say that Conestoga had been gone?'

'Four hours. But it's carrying a heavy load, and mules ain't the fastest creatures. I reckon, what, four or five miles an hour? At best that puts it twenty miles ahead of us.'

'But it's still moving away from us. What bothers me is that at any time in those four hours, and in the time it takes us to catch up, Gamboa and the Coogans could've pounced.'

'That's true. Them, or those two ex-cons.'

Carson snorted. 'Forget ex-cons. I'm after Gamboa – and so are you, though I'm still not sure why.'

He glanced across. Creed was mostly looking straight ahead into the moonlit distance, only occasionally leaning sideways in the saddle and studying the trail to make sure they were still riding in the Conestoga's ruts. He gave no reaction at all to Carson's open invitation to tell more of his story.

'If Gamboa's already hit that wagon,' Carson went on, 'we've lost him.'

'That would indeed be bad,' Creed said. 'I came to Yuma and you gave me hope. I'd hate to have that dashed because we foolishly went off chasing the wrong wagon.'

'Hope is about all I've ever had,' Carson said.

As they began riding through a stand of trees that closed in on the trail so that they were riding between dark walls of evergreen, he flicked another glance at his companion. 'You told me about a Mex bandit telling gruesome tales, but you never did explain why that made you throw in your badge—'

'Look, there's been trouble here,' Creed said.

He'd pulled his horse back to a walk. Now he drew rein and sprang down. When Carson turned back and dismounted the tall man was walking to and fro, head bent as he studied the ground. The tall trees rearing high on either side were turning the trail into a passage beyond the reach of the moon's rays, yet despite the gloom Carson could see that where before there had been clear ruts proceeding in an easterly direction along the Oxbow route, now the earth was churned by wheels and hoofs moving in all directions.

'There was a second wagon,' Creed said as he prowled. 'Here' – he gestured – 'it was broadside across the trail. Then, see here: the Conestoga's ruts come right up to it. But now, just here, these splintered branches and deep ruts in the softer earth show that the Conestoga was manoeuvred so it was off the trail – and now, clearly, the wagon that was broadside on swings round and heads back towards Yuma.'

'You read sign better than me,' Carson said, 'but what makes you say trouble? Sounds like the Conestoga came upon that second wagon, and had to get out of the way so it could pass.'

'No, there was something else,' Creed said. 'A way back, when we were talking, I'm certain we passed a place where the Conestoga was overtaken by another wagon that was half off the trail as it went by.'

'You said nothing.'

'I wasn't sure. Or if I was, I couldn't see any connection. But now this' – he made a broad, sweeping gesture – 'this tells a clear story.'

'Yeah.' Carson swung into the saddle and watched Creed as he walked on down the trail, still examining tracks. 'A wagon passed the Conestoga, pulled ahead, then swung around to block the trail.'

'And after that,' Creed called, 'the Conestoga went on its way.'

He walked back to his horse, mounted, and rejoined Carson.

'Only reason for anyone stopping the Conestoga is to get the gold,' he said. 'But these signs tell only part of a story. We need to know who did this. Was it Gamboa and the Coogans, or the two ex-cons. Whoever it was, did they get the gold?'

'Yeah, and what the hell do we do now?' Carson said bitterly. 'We've chased one wagon today and got nothing for our trouble. I'd hate to do the same again.'

'Damn right. But the problem we're facing,' Creed said, swinging his horse to the west, 'is the only way to get the answer to any of those questions is to press on. There's nothing else we can do.'

Half an hour later it was the two horses that sensed more serious trouble as Carson and Creed came up behind a Conestoga wagon that was standing half in another stand of dark trees, leaning drunkenly to the left. Their mounts' ears went up. Suddenly they were holding back, tossing their heads as they tried to turn away.

'They smell something,' Carson said. 'Only one thing I know would make them act this skittish.'

'Yeah, and I don't think it's those mules.'

Creed was already swinging out of the saddle and tying his horse to the nearest tree. Carson did the same, then hurried to catch up with the tall man who was jogging towards the wagon with his six-gun in his hand.

As he drew nearer, Carson's nostrils twitched. He could smell gunsmoke and, very faintly, there something else; a sickly smell he recognized, one that always had the power to turn a man's stomach and make him think darkly of his own mortality.

'Both dead?' he queried.

The wagon was rocking as the mules, tangled in the traces, tried to back away from the two men. Creed was up on the wagon's boot. He was bent over two still bodies. The smell of fresh blood was stronger. He turned his head to look at Carson, grabbed a hold as the mules snorted and the wagon lurched. The look in his eyes was at once one of horror, and of intense excitement.

'The closest I've been,' he said in a voice quivering with tension. 'Closest you've been, too, I'll warrant. Yes, they're dead, both of them – and like Sorensen said, they're young fellows barely in their twenties.'

'What makes you say we're close?'

'If I come across someone with his skin sliced by a knife and I know Gamboa's in the area, I'm already halfway convinced he was responsible. When the slicing takes the shape of his initial – the letter L – then I know damn well I'm right. He's been here. This is his handiwork.'

Creed leaped down, pouched his pistol. For a moment he hesitated, frowning. Then he strode to the rear of the wagon and climbed inside. He emerged seconds later, shaking his head. He took a deep breath. When he let it out, some of the excitement went with it.

'Sacks of grain. They've been split open. Gamboa and those Irish sons of bitches must have been looking for the gold, but those sacks are full, no space in any of them for cash in any form. If I'm reading this right then they went away empty-handed—'

'How is the cargo distributed? How much space do those sacks take up? And have they been moved around?'

'What are you getting at?'

'There's no gold in those sacks, there's no gold anywhere in the wagon. I think the sacks of grain were a cargo put there to hide the gold.'

'And now it's gone?'

'That's right.'

Creed grimaced. 'So who took it? The boys in that second wagon who stopped this one way back down the trail? Or was it taken here, by Gamboa and his pals?'

Carson took off his hat, scratched his head. He looked back down the trail, frowning. Then his face cleared as he looked at Creed.

'No, I think you're right: Gamboa and the Coogans left empty handed. Only reason those sacks would be split is if the searchers couldn't find the gold. Only reason they wouldn't be able to find the gold is if it had already been taken.'

'By the boys using that second wagon – and they'd have to be those two ex-cons, right?'

But still Carson wasn't satisfied. He knew that they could mull over all the possibilities and decide that one of them was obvious, and therefore correct. But could they be sure?

He looked at Creed, and shook his head.

'There is another possibility.'

'I know.' Creed looked keenly at Carson. 'You're talking about a double bluff?'

'Yes. Whoever's behind this – politicians, army

personnel, the United States government – could have shrewdly put themselves in the outlaws' place, decided they'd figure the escort had been put with an empty wagon to fool them. If they did, then they got it absolutely right. Those two ex-cons, and Gamboa and the Coogans, ignored that wagon with the escort and went after this one, when all the time the gold's in the wagon with the escort.'

'Where?'

Carson shrugged. 'I'd say they slung a canvas underneath that first Conestoga. That's where the money is.'

'And the rifles?'

'Genuine. They'll be delivered to Fort Huachuca, like the man said.'

Now it was Creed who was shaking his head.

'You said "could have": the politicians or other big wigs "could have" put themselves inside the outlaws' heads, "could have" worked a double bluff. But we don't know that, we *can't* know that.'

'So where does that leave us?'

'Right now,' Creed said, 'we've got two dead men, a Conestoga wagon loaded with sacks of grain and no idea what to do next.'

PART THREE

THIRTEEN

On the long, rattling night drive back to La Buena Tierra, Kade and Hood exchanged not a single word. There was an electric tension between them, a tension that, though they were physically close on the wagon's boot, kept them apart and alone with their thoughts. Each man covertly watched the other, each struggling to deal in his own way with the turmoil that churned within and left him searching for answers.

Hood was holding the makeshift traces lightly, working the two saddle horses like a team, for most of the way managing to keep the creaking wagon in the centre of the trail. They splashed across the Gila River's wide ford leaving a trail of glittering moonlit spray and, as they pushed on towards the foothills, the pale dawn lightening the broad spread of the eastern skies began washing the slopes of the Castle Dome mountains with pastel shades of pink and pale yellow.

Kade spoke first, talking through his teeth as Hood guided the wagon off the trail and onto the drive in to La Buena Tierra.

'How long d'you plan on stopping here?'

'As long as it takes us to decide what to do,' Hood said. Then he cast a fierce glance at Kade. 'You . . . well, I guess you want to pull out now?'

'I didn't say that.'

'I'm reading the signs. Lord knows I did enough of it in the pen – enough to keep me alive when trouble was brewing. But if I'm wrong about your plans, let me know. We've worked together well enough up to now, and the way things stand I need all the help I can get.' He grinned coldly. 'Like I said at the outset, on that first day when we walked down the hill from the jail, we need each other.'

They left the empty wagon at an angle under the ranch's perilously hanging name board, freed their horses from the ropes tying them to the single- and double-trees and rode them the rest of the way into the ranch yard. There they left them, loosely tied to the rail, cinches slackened but saddles still in place.

'No sense getting over confident,' Hood said.

Kade shrugged, slung his saddle-bags over his shoulder and with his rifle in the other hand, walked up the steps onto the gallery and kicked open the front door. From what they had noticed on their previous visit he had expected to see signs of recent occupation, and sure enough it was obvious that several men had eaten around the large table.

He dumped the saddle-bags, propped his rifle against the wall and set to work. Within minutes he had a fire crackling in the big pot-bellied stove, and what was left of the provisions they had picked up on the first day of freedom in Yuma sizzling in a flat black skillet. He found tin plates, slid the hot food onto two of them and carried them across to the table.

Hood had his back to the room. He was standing looking out of the cracked window and across the yard to where they had left the wagon. When he turned and sat down, his eyes were gleaming.

'So, if we couldn't find that gold,' he said, 'where is it?'

'It never was on that wagon,' Kade said, speaking around a mouthful of greasy bacon. 'The driver told us they were carrying grain, and he was speaking the truth. What's more, when we mentioned gold he had no idea what we were talking about.'

'I know.' Hood nodded, poked at his food with a knife, shook his head. 'The question was academic, Kade. We both know where the money is, we just don't like admitting it because it makes us look like a couple of fools.'

'We followed the wrong wagon,' Kade said bluntly. He put down his fork and began rolling a cigarette. 'The one we should've followed headed south. By now it's reached the Mex border and—'

'And what? The military escort makes it untouchable? It's already travelled too far and is beyond our reach? Or because of those factors – one or all of 'em – we're already way too late, or too damn timid ever to get our sticky hands on that gold?'

There was a challenge in Hood's voice and in those shining eyes. Kade met that gaze and something in him stirred. He knew at once that Hood was deliberately goading him, and was startled to realize that the big man's ploy was working. The acute disappointment he had felt when, out there in the dark on the Oxbow route they realized they had held up a wagon carrying supplies of grain, was rapidly fading. His thoughts had become focused when, half listening to Hood's words, he tried mentally to follow that first Conestoga's route. And, by God, it was far too early to admit that they were too late.

The incongruity of those final thoughts caused his lips to twitch in a grin.

'No,' he said quietly, 'it's not beyond our reach. If that Conestoga's reached the Mex border and turned east, we can cut it off by riding across country. In some ways this delay could be to our advantage. The further that wagon travels without hitting trouble, the more relaxed those horse soldiers will be. When we do hit them, we'll have the element of surprise—'

'So you're in?'

'I was never out,' Kade said. 'From the first day this has been about retribution. We're owed for the time we spent in jail. Someone's going to pay for that, and we won't make them pay by sitting here jawing—'

Behind Hood, the window's cracked glass shattered.

The glittering fragments were still flying, deadly razor-sharp shards, when Kade rolled out of his chair and hit the floor. Hood was already down, scrabbling across the floor towards the window, one hand fumbling for his six-gun.

A second shot followed the first. Splinters flew from a high sideboard. And then a hail of bullets poured through the window, dust and splinters flew and, ears ringing, senses spinning, Kade and Hood were effectively pinned to the floor.

It was Gamboa, the 'breed, who took on the task of locating the site of the first ambush and following the wagon they had been told was carrying the gold.

When the Conestoga driver died he left the three outlaws with little more than the knowledge that the gold had gone – but that little more was enough. If the gold had been transferred from one wagon to another, it must have happened on the trail between Yuma and Agua Caliente where Gamboa and the Coogans had staged their abortive ambush. So it was with haste, yet considerable circumspection, that the outlaws left the stranded Conestoga and the two dead men and pointed their horses back towards Yuma.

The circumspection paid off. They had gone less than a mile when Gamboa's sharp ears caught the sound of approaching riders and the three outlaws pulled off the trail. From the depths of shadows cast by the high moon they peered through shifting, clicking branches and watched with nervous hands clutching six-guns. Two men rode by, in a hurry. Neither of them was recognized by Gamboa or the Coogans.

Where they lawmen? If so, who where they hunting? Gamboa was naturally cautious, but in Mick Coogan's opinion who they were and what they were doing was of no consequence. They pushed on, and ten minutes later they were riding across tracks that criss-crossed the trail, and on either side they could see the white were

103

wagons being manoeuvred had snapped whole branches from the trees.

'It was here,' Gamboa said. 'Two wagons, one across the trail this way, the other coming up fast and heading towards Agua Caliente. It stops – see, the mules, they kick up the dirt, the wagon slides. And then it changes. This wagon, the one pulled by mules, is moved off the trail. Then it continues – we know that, because a little later we stopped it and when we confronted the young driver and his guard a little blood was shed.'

'Vicious bastard,' Bren Coogan said.

Slouched in the saddle, sombrero tilted back, Gamboa was grinning darkly.

'Ah yes,' he said, 'that may be true, but without me—'

'Don't need you, even I can read what's happened here. The other wagon turns and heads back. But to where? It's got the stolen gold on board. Mick, can you see it going all the way into Yuma?'

Mick shook his head. 'Wouldn't risk it. Somewhere between here and town it'll turn off.'

'And then, you see, I will come to the rescue,' Gamboa said. 'When it comes to tracking I have the necessary skill—'

'Jesus Christ,' Brendan Coogan said, 'will you give it a rest?'

Nevertheless, even Bren Coogan was very soon forced to admit that they did need Gamboa. They had proceeded for another couple of miles when the 'breed proved it to them craftily by allowing them to ride beyond the point where the wagon carrying the gold had turned off the trail, then loftily informing them that they had gone too far.

'It went that way,' he said, as the three men gathered at the spot where he had noticed the sign. 'They are now heading north. Very soon after this they must ford the Gila.'

'Does that sound familiar to you?' Brendan said, and his brother nodded.

'I was thinking the same thing.'

'Familiar, yes, but is it likely they started from the same place we did?'

'There was a wagon there, at that run-down homestead,' Mick said. 'If you remember, we thought of using it ourselves but decided it was too far gone to be of use.'

'And maybe it was and we're dreaming,' Brendan said, 'but in my time I have had the most unlikely dreams turn out to be true.'

Gamboa was naturally superstitious. He listened with growing excitement, and expressed the opinion that after snatching away the glittering prize the fates had now relented and were looking on them favourably.

'You will see,' he said, as they cut away from the trail and headed at a canter towards the smell of fresh water. 'We will follow these ruts and they will lead to La Buena Tierra.'

'You sound mighty certain,' Mick said.

'I am one hundred per cent certain because I can see with my eyes that there are ruts going in both directions. The wagon came this way, and it is returning. It is following its own tracks.'

'But not necessarily to La Buena Tierra.'

Yet by now all three men were living in hope. The broken down ranch was on familiar territory, was itself a home from home where many times they had holed up. They were also recalling the words of the dying driver. The money had been taken by two men. And two men, taken by surprise, were unlikely to cause them much trouble.

It was through the pale light of dawn that Lope Gamboa and the Coogans approached La Buena Tierra. They were still half a mile away from the ruined buildings and riding in what cover they could find by keeping to the sparse trees when Mick Coogan pulled his horse to a halt and spoke up.

'The wagon's there,' he said, 'but it's been moved.'

'Damn it, we've got them,' Bren said gleefully.

'Almost. We know they're here, now we figure out how to take them.'

'Fire power. We've got three rifles. We move in close, two of us keep their heads down with continuous fire while the other moves up to the house. When he's flat against the walls, a second follows, again under covering fire.'

'If they are watching right now,' Gamboa warned, 'we will not get even close enough to fire the first shot.'

There was truth in what he said, for between their present position and the house there was no natural cover. Knowing that the two men with stolen government money were likely to be in a highly nervous state, the Coogans opted to ride a wide arc around the corral which would bring them in behind the derelict barn. They were about to begin that risky move when

Gamboa hissed a warning.

'I see someone, at the window.'

'He's looking out,' Bren Coogan said, shading his eyes as he squinted into the distance. 'Damn. As long as he stays there, we're stuck.'

'So we wait. They're not going anywhere either.'

'Then I am mystified,' Gamboa said. 'You say they are not going anywhere, and that troubles me. The wagon also troubles me. If they used that for the gold, they would not leave it there unless they have taken the gold into the house. But why would they do that? In the house the gold is of no use to them.'

'I see the second man,' Bren said suddenly. He'd pulled a battered pair of field-glasses from his saddle-bag and was studying the house. 'Moving about the room.'

'And me, I am hungry and for sure I smell something cooking,' said Lope Gamboa.

'If a meal's being dished up he won't stay at the window too long. Yes, now' – Bren whipped the glasses away from his eyes and spun around – 'that second man's sat down, the other fellow's turned away from the window—'

'All right,' Mick said, 'let's move.'

With Mick leading and Bren snatching the occasional glance at the house through the glasses they rode the three-quarter mile half-circle that took them around the corral and brought them up against the rear wall of the barn.

After that they moved quickly; the dust kicked up by their approach was hanging in the air and at any moment could give them away.

Swiftly they tied the horses to the corral's rail. Then the three outlaws slipped into the barn and took cover behind bales of hay, barrels, the remains of the walls – anything or anywhere they could find.

Lope Gamboa volunteered to make the first run.

'I get there, to the house, maybe I don't stop,' he said. 'Maybe I go straight in, use my knife, it's all over—'

'Cut the talk, get to it,' Mick Coogan snarled.

Gamboa looped a dirty forefinger through a fine gold chain at his throat, pulled out a gold crucifix and pressed it to his lips. Then he let the cross fall, slipped out his knife and gripped it between strong white teeth.

Mick nodded to Brendan. Both men lifted their rifle and took aim. Then they opened fire. Across the yard the window shattered. As the first glittering fragments of glass fell, Lope Gamboa set off towards the house at a crouching, zig-zagging run.

With bullets flying within inches of his head, the 'breed made it across the yard. His sombrero slipped to his shoulders, held there by its silken cord. He reached the canted gallery, leaped up and ran through the ragged overgrowth of grass towards the front door.

Mick Coogan stopped firing, tilted his rifle.

'Will you look at him! That son of a bitch 'breed's keeping his word. He's going straight in.'

FOURTEEN

Frank Carson and Joe Creed rode into Yuma with the sun rising and sending their long shadows creeping ahead of them down the main street. Their horses' heads were hanging wearily. Both Carson and Creed were heavy eyed, aching in every joint, and craving for a hot meal and a few hours' rest.

But it was indecision that had brought them all the way back down the Oxbow route, and that indecision was haunting them, refusing to let them pause in their endeavours. They were hunting the man called Lope Gamboa. The bloody crime they had discovered at Agua Caliente led them to believe that they had been within hours, perhaps minutes, of catching him. But like a wraith, the murderous 'breed had slipped away into the night, and the puzzle left behind remained unsolved. Where was the gold? Had it been taken, and if so by whom?

Those were questions that they were too tired to attempt to answer. They desperately needed advice, or at the very least a morsel of news that would enable them to formulate a plan that might have a slim chance of working. And, as they rode down Yuma's main street, the light that was still glowing in the window of Lars Sorensen's office gave them hope.

They dismounted wearily, tied their horses and stamped up onto the plank walk. When the entered the office, Sorensen was rising from his swivel chair.

'Any luck?'

'Depends how you interpret the word,' Carson said, sinking into a chair. 'We reckon we've run across more of Gamboa's brutal work, but if we have it's not yet done us any good.'

'The wagon on the Oxbow route was ambushed, driver and guard murdered and mutilated in a way that points to Gamboa,' Creed explained. He'd spun a chair in his big hands and was straddling it, his folded arms resting on the back. 'Unfortunately, there was no sign of any gold. We're trying to work out what happened to it. Could be Gamboa and the Coogans got their hands on it, which means Gamboa's long gone.'

'I can't tell you where he is,' Sorensen said, 'but I do know he hasn't got the gold because it was never on that wagon.'

Both Carson and Creed stared at the Yuma marshal. Carson was the first to speak. His mind was dulled by weariness, but despite that he felt a sudden prickle of excitement.

'You've had more news?'

Sorensen nodded. 'Came in overnight. I've been in touch with colleagues of mine over the border in California. They've not only brought me up to date

110

with the Southern Pacific's troubles, they were able to dig deep and get to the bottom of this gold fiasco.'

'We've had our own thoughts about that,' Carson said. 'Be interesting to hear if we got it right.'

'Oh, it's not complicated. One thing led to another. You already know about the landslip that halted the railroad. When that blocked the way through it was decided to bypass the fault by moving the gold by road. They knew there was a military wagon in the vicinity. It was taking rifles to Fort Huachuca. They used that.'

'They?'

Sorensen shrugged. 'That's the bit nobody's prepared to talk about. What I gather is the gold is urgently needed by government departments back East. The delay caused by the landslip would have been more than unacceptable, it would have been disastrous.'

'Dammit,' Carson breathed. 'I can't believe we've been close to the gold, and close to Gamboa, and come out of it with nothing.'

Sorensen nodded. 'Yeah, you went after the right wagon first time but those cavalry boys managed to fool you, then you missed Gamboa by a whisker.'

'Out there on the trail we sort of worked out what was going on,' Creed said, 'but it seems like we rode halfway across Arizona to do it.'

'That's true, so what about the second wagon?' Carson said. 'Was that part of a double bluff?'

Sorensen shook his head. 'Keep it simple, because that's what they did. The second wagon was a simple decoy: they sent it out with instructions to take the

Oxbow route, and used that journalist to announce it in the newspaper. By doing that they hoped the other wagon carrying rifles and gold would slip through unnoticed.'

'I wish it had,' Carson said ruefully. 'If we'd gone after the decoy wagon we might have been there when Gamboa made his move.'

'If he hasn't given up, and I don't think he will,' Sorensen said, 'you should make sure you're there when he tries again. He's murdered once for that gold, he'll surely keep after it.'

'Maybe.' Carson grimaced. 'But that wagon's got too much start on us, and by coming back to Yuma we've put ourselves in the wrong place. From here, we'll be chasing the wagon; from the ambush site at Agua Caliente, Gamboa and his pals can ride across country and cut it off – hell, they're probably already on their way.'

'But if he does, and bests that cavalry escort,' Sorensen pointed out, 'he'll be stuck with the wagon. You'll still be chasing it, but it'll have a different driver: Gamboa, the man you're both hunting; and, flushed with success, he'll be overconfident.'

'I've just had a nasty thought,' Carson said, glancing across at Creed.

'Yeah, me too. It's hard on that cavalry escort, but there's no doubt we stand a far better chance of catching Gamboa if he does take over that wagon.'

The realization that if Gamboa succeeded in stealing the gold he would be slowed down and made more vulnerable took some of the pressure off Carson and Creed. Carson knew that if the opposite occurred and Gamboa failed, then he would be as far away as ever from capture, but Sorensen's parting shot made him quietly sanguine: Lope Gamboa, in Sorenson's opinion, was not going to give up.

When the two men left the marshal's office they quickly discovered that a hot bath was nowhere available. The next priority was a meal, and there they had better luck: the greasy café next to the saloon had a policy of remaining open until the last customer left, and five minutes after walking in and ordering they were sitting down to a huge fry up of beef, onion, potatoes washed down by as much coffee as they could drink.

Fifteen minutes after that they were sitting back, replete, enjoying a relaxing cigarette.

Contemplating his tall companion and recalling his earlier tale, Frank Carson was again unable to resist pressing for more details.

'I asked you back there on the trail,' he said, 'but things more urgent took over. As far as it goes the tale you told already is about as good as any I've heard in a long time, but there's too much been left out. As I'm helping you go after this Gamboa it's only right—'

'Whoa there,' Creed said. 'You and your partner were doing the hunting long before I arrived on the scene. From where I stand that suggests it's me doing the helping.'

'Fair enough, but you *know* why I'm after that bloodthirsty 'breed. All I know is you overheard a story told by a Mex bandit.'

'If you give it some thought,' Creed said, 'you'll realize the answer's there in both our stories.'

'What – they're linked?'

'Sure they are.'

Carson frowned, rocked back in his chair, blew smoke at the ceiling. The door slammed and a bell tinkled as a satisfied customer went out into the lamp-lit street.

'So what have we got?' Carson mused. 'A tale of rape and pillage on your side, on my side knowledge of a Mex renegade working with Indians who murdered a family, took a young boy. . . .'

He stopped and stared at Creed.

'The boy wasn't taken,' Creed said.

'Because that boy is you?'

Creed nodded.

'So . . . what was it? The Indians rode in, Gamboa with them, they attacked the house and you managed to hide?'

'I was in the barn. I wriggled under the straw, wet my pants as I listened with my hands over my ears to the screams of my mother and my sister. When all went quiet, when darkness was creeping in and I was shivering with cold, I crawled out of my hiding place and I took the only broken down pony they'd left and I rode away from there.'

'Jesus,' Carson said softly. 'You didn't—'

'Go into the house? See if anyone in there was alive?' Creed shook his head. 'I was twelve years old. I couldn't handle it, and that cowardice has been haunting me ever since.'

'Unnecessarily,' Carson said. 'In similar circumstances, strong men have acted in the same way.'

Creed pushed his plate away. 'Maybe now you understand why an overheard conversation made me pack in my job and hit the trail.'

'You bet your boots I do. Hell, I seethe with anger every time I think of what those ex-cons did to my partner – and that's as nothing compared to the memories you've carried with you for all those years.' He scraped his chair back and stepped away from the table. 'Well, those ex-cons may be out of the picture and too far away for me to touch, but for you the time is approaching when an ageing Mex bandit is going to have to pay for his sins. There's a long ride ahead of us, and we can't be sure what we'll encounter at the end of it—'

'We'll find Gamboa,' Creed said firmly. 'He's not going to give up. Somehow he'll find out where he went wrong, find his way to the gold. You mark my words. That yellow gold will attract him the way a yellow flame attracts a moth.'

'You're sure of that?'

'I'm certain.'

'And you're prepared to make that long ride now, even though we've had no sleep?'

'I would willingly sleep round the clock. But in that time, how many more miles would the Conestoga gain?'

'Too damn many, considering how far ahead it is already,' Carson said. 'But, as the Texas Rangers were somewhat lax when your family was being murdered, I feel duty bound to help you all I can. Come on, feller, let's ride into the sun and see if you're right about finding Gamboa.'

FIFTEEN

As the door crashed open and Lope Gamboa charged into the derelict house, knife between his teeth and a pistol held high in his right hand, Bren and Mick Coogan ceased firing. A terrible silence settled over the yard. So intense was the quiet that Mick could hear his pulse thundering, the heavy breathing of the man who was standing several yards away.

'Far as we know there's two men in there,' Bren said, a puzzled frown on his face. 'They've stolen a wagonload of gold and I can't believe one man can burst in with a knife and handgun and take the two of them without a goddamn fight—'

He broke off, visibly jumped as a shot rang out, then a second. It was followed by another aching silence, and Bren looked across at his brother. There was a question in his eyes, but it was one Mick could not answer. He squinted across the yard then held up a hand.

'Well, look at that,' he said quietly.

A rifle had been poked through the half open door. From the muzzle a white cloth dangled. Then a man

117

stepped out. He was tall, powerfully built. Despite the symbolic white flag there was no hint of defeat in his demeanour. Even from across the broad expanse of the yard the Coogans could see the brash confidence in his gaze. He stood there, the rifle butt resting on his hip, the weapon jutting at what might be a jaunty angle, and with infinite patience he waited in the bright sunlight for a reaction.

'That's a flag of surrendering he's holding,' Bren said, disbelief in his voice, 'but a man less inclined to give up the fight I have yet to see.'

'Nevertheless, if he's standing there waving that damn rag there's one thing we know with absolute certainty, and that's that Gamboa is dead.'

'No great loss,' Bren said, 'having that bloodthirsty devil out of the way, but it does create complications.'

'About which we'd better do something.'

'With caution.' Bren gestured with his rifle. 'Gamboa's down. I have sometimes seen a flag of surrender used to lure the unwary onto waiting guns – and, as we know, there's two of them, that window we poured our fire into is a wonderful opening from which to gun down the unwary.'

The man on the gallery through whose warped boards the wild grass sprouted called out mockingly, 'I always knew the Irish could talk the hind legs off a donkey,' he said, 'but I didn't have them down for lacking in courage. You should trust this flag. My companion and I have a proposition to make. As it concerns gold which, as we speak, is moving further and further away from us, I don't think you should spend too long looking for a trap. There is none. The offer is a straightforward deal. Come on over.'

After once more exchanging glances with his brother, Mick Coogan shrugged and stepped from the barn into the dust of the yard. He kept the rifle across his body, his finger crooked around the trigger. As he began the walk across open space, he was aware of Bren doing the same but moving well away to his right so that they were separated and would present two difficult targets.

In the event, there was no trickery. They reached the gallery and stepped up onto the creaking boards and, as their boots brushed through the wild grass, the man with the flag of surrender stepped to one side to let them through.

Mick Coogan shook his head.

'After you, my friend. We've listened to two shots being fired, and a Mexican *compadre* of ours is unusually silent. Presenting you with our backs is not an option.'

The big man shrugged, and stepped into the house.

Mick Coogan gestured to his brother to stay outside and move across to the window, then followed the man with the white flag. He walked into a bare room containing little more than a stove and a table. The stove's iron was creaking as it cooled. Greasy plates were lying on the table. Glittering shards of glass littered the floor, the result of the Coogans' intense fusillade that had, it seemed, achieved nothing.

At the rear of the room an open door led to the back yard which was bounded by a broken-down fence. Beyond that, rough grassland stretched away to the opposite slope of the broad canyon. Mick Coogan stopped in his tracks. As he realized what he was looking at, his eyes narrowed and he wondered, perhaps a little too late, if he had walked into a trap.

The tall man with the rag tied to his rifle had stepped to one side. He had made no threatening moves, and Coogan's disquiet eased slightly. But another man was dragging the body of Lope Gamboa towards the open back door. He was dragging the 'breed by his feet. Gamboa's colourful sombrero was scraping across the floor behind him. The man and his burden reached the door. Without hesitation, Gamboa was dragged through the doorway. There were several steps. His limp body went down in jerks, his head banging on each step. At the bottom the man pulling him gave a final heave, then let go. Contemptuously dusting his hands, he stepped back inside and closed the door.

'And now,' the tall man said, 'we can discuss a certain consignment of gold.'

'First, let's get some kind of equality into the situation,' Mick Coogan said. He looked towards the window and called, 'Come on in, Bren. Gamboa's finished, but keep your finger on the trigger and your eye on these two when you walk in through the door.'

'Not very trusting,' said the tall man.

'Put yourself in my place,' Mick Coogan said, 'then thank the good Lord I'm even talking to you.'

The tall man nodded his understanding. 'I'm Deakin Hood,' he said. 'The man you saw disposing of the body of Lope Gamboa is Adam Kade. We were recently kicked out of the Yuma Pen. Like all convicts, we have for years been complaining bitterly that we were wrongly convicted. In our case – and whether you believe it is entirely up to you – it's true: we did not commit the crimes for which we were imprisoned. And so, when we were released, we vowed to get even. Stealing the consignment of gold I'm sure you both read about in the newspapers seemed a good way to start.'

'According to the driver of the Conestoga wagon,' Bren Coogan said, standing just inside the door with his rifle covering the group, 'you've already managed to do that.'

'He was wrong—'

'There was no gold in the wagon, and when the driver spoke he was dying,' Mick Coogan said. 'Why would he lie?'

'If he was dying, why not?' Hood said. 'It was a final act of defiance; he was metaphorically spitting in your eye. But, more importantly, he was doing what he'd been paid for and buying time for the second Conestoga wagon.'

For a moment there was silence. Deakin Hood studied the Coogans' faces. Then he nodded slowly and smiled.

'I thought so,' he said to Adam Kade. 'That's the first the infamous Coogans have heard of another wagon.'

'Gamboa chose the ambush site,' Mick Coogan said. 'The first we saw of any wagon was when it approached Agua Caliente in the moonlight and Gamboa blasted the driver and guard with his shotgun.'

'You'd gone too far down the trail,' Adam Kade said

bluntly. 'We waited and watched on the outskirts of Yuma. A Conestoga wagon came through and headed south, two cavalrymen riding escort. We let that wagon go. A second came soon after and turned onto the Oxbow route – exactly as predicted in the newspaper article, so of course that was the one we followed. When we stopped it, we discovered our mistake.'

'So why come here?'

'Let's say we're honest men, and wished to return the borrowed wagon.' He grinned. 'Look, consider our being here as a gift from the gods. Gamboa was a liability. We've done you a favour by getting rid of a wild, bloodthirsty 'breed who could turn even the best laid plans into blueprints for disaster. We've told you where the gold is: I think you can guess what comes next.'

'The flag you waved means you've no appetite for a fight.'

'With you, no. Fighting with you gets us nothing.'

'There's nothing to be gained by teaming up with us – if it's that you're suggesting.'

'It is. Four men stand a better chance than two when there's a military escort to be overcome.'

'Even if we agree, there's still a problem. You've told us the direction that wagon took, but south is too broad a concept. It could mean anywhere. I can see us wasting days, weeks, looking for a small needle in a very large haystack.'

'Would that wagon, with a US military escort, head south and cross the Mexican border?'

'No, it could not do that.'

'We know it headed south. Before it reaches the border it must turn again and head east. It's a lumbering Conestoga wagon, crossing rough terrain. We are four men on fast horses. I put it to you: do you think that by riding across country we might cut it off?'

Mick looked at his brother, saw the slow nod.

'I think there's a damn good chance,' he said.

'And you'd agree to a sixty/forty split?'

'In our favour?'

Hood grinned. 'You tried for the gold, and got nothing. We've offered you hope, but it comes at a price.'

'Sure, and I know the effect gold can have on a man,' Mick Coogan said. 'No matter what is said here, when that gold is in our hands any agreements made stand for nothing. I foresee men going wild, I foresee bloodshed—'

'You're turning down the offer?'

'I'm saying we go with you, we stop that wagon, together we take the gold. After that' – Mick Coogan shrugged – 'after that, who finally gets to hold on to the gold is, as they say, in the lap of the gods. It is highly likely the identity of the person left in possession will be decided not by agreements honoured, nor by the roll of a dice, but by the accuracy or otherwise of the man who's first to draw his six-gun.'

'Better to be that close and fighting, than countless miles away from riches and doing nothing,' Deakin Hood said. 'But I can tell you this: if we do fight amongst ourselves over the gold, it will be one hell of a battle.'

'What happens, happens,' Bren Coogan said enigmatically. 'But I have one last proposal, and it's this: when we have downed those military men, we exchange clothing with them. That way, when the Conestoga wagon drives on it will leave dead outlaws lying on the trail, the brave, triumphant cavalrymen still riding escort.'

SIXTEEN

The world, Lope Gamboa thought, was a curious and unpredictable place which never ceased to amaze.

One hot morning in a one-horse Arizona town to the west of Casa Grandé he had picked up a newspaper and discovered that a large quantity of government gold was about to cross his path; it was to be driven along the old Oxbow route in a vulnerable Conestoga wagon, a red rag of immense riches dangled before snorting outlaw bulls. It was a challenge he could not resist, Gamboa had decided, and so he had devised a plan. That plan involved the use of other men; with them he would embark on a violent course of action which would see the quantity of gold falling into their hands, and after that successful outcome he would execute the perfect double-cross so that all of the gold would be his.

When he managed to inveigle the Coogan brothers into going along with him, all, it seemed, was settled; yet such was the unpredictability of life that at a late stage, when the plan had already swung into action, something so unexpected occurred that it made every one of his carefully considered decisions meaningless.

Or perhaps, Gamboa mused, not all of them. His plan, in its essentials, had been sound, but he had been unwise when choosing his armed companions. The Coogan brothers, he had very quickly realized, would not be easy to double-cross. They were hard men, and worldly wise. In their eyes he had seen an understanding of what he, Gamboa was planning; and it had at once occurred to him that not only was he using them, but they were using him.

He had been faced with a dilemma, and could see no satisfactory way out.

Then the unexpected had occurred: the government gold had been snatched by other men. The wagon had followed its predicted route, the ambush with the Coogans had gone smoothly and according to plan, but when the wagon's canvas was lifted, the gold had miraculously been turned into useless sacks of grain.

Or so it seemed, Gamboa thought, chuckling at the memory.

But, no, there had been two men, the dying driver had said, blood dribbling from his lips as he spoke. Half an hour earlier and a few miles back down the trail it was they who had taken the gold. They had transferred it to a second wagon, and driven away into the night.

Very soon, and not too many miles later, Gamboa had discovered to his amazement that one of those men was Deakin Hood.

Sitting on a log in the yard at the rear of the derelict house, Lope Gamboa smiled a contented smile.

From the site of the abortive ambush he and the

126

Coogans had ridden to La Buena Tierra. Leaving the brothers in the barn he had crossed the yard, burst into the house with his knife between his teeth and a six-gun in his hand, and had been confronted by a tall man who was pointing a cocked rifle at his belly. In that instant, death for both of them was but a split second away. Luckily, recognition had been instantaneous, reactions commendably swift. Trigger fingers had been stayed and, as the seconds crawled by in silence, and across the yard the Coogan brothers waited impatiently for Gamboa to go to work with gun and knife, another plan had been devised.

Hood and his companion did not have the missing gold, but the mystery of its whereabouts had been solved. The wagon carrying it was guarded by the US Cavalry. In return for his help, they were willing to share their knowledge and the riches.

Hood's plan, swiftly concocted, was to go after the gold with the Coogans, and for the supposedly dead Gamboa to follow at a distance. The four men – Hood, Kade and the Coogans – would attack the Conestoga wagon, overpower the cavalry escort and seize the wagon and gold. Then Gamboa would show himself, and with Hood and Kade supporting him the Coogan brothers would be gunned down.

Lope Gamboa was more than happy to accept the generous offer. If the Coogan brothers were hard men, both Hood and his companion were crafty, but weak. They were losers who had spent years in prison. Once the gold had been seized and the two Irish outlaws dealt with, double-crossing Hood and Kade would,

Gamboa knew, be an undertaking well within his capabilities and without any risk.

Agreement had been reached. Deakin Hood had drawn his six-gun and fired two shots into the dirt floor. It had brought Mick Coogan running across the gallery in time to witness Hood's companion, Adam Kade, dragging the 'dead' 'breed through the back door.

When the back door slammed Gamboa had lain where Kade had dragged him, quite comfortable in the early morning sun. He had listened as Hood and Kade had arranged a shaky partnership with Mick and Bren Coogan, then climbed to his feet as he heard footsteps stamp out of the house and, moments later, hoofbeats fade into the distance.

From that moment, he took his time. He had heard Hood and Kade telling the Coogans about the wagon that had turned right after leaving Yuma and headed south. His knife and six-gun had been left where he had dropped them. His horse was still tethered behind the barn. His gleaming Winchester rifle was safely tucked in the supple leather boot under the saddle fender.

He knew where he was going, and he knew exactly how a reasonably complicated plot and counter-plot would turn a half-Mexican peasant into a rich man.

He had set out to use other men. Now those other men were riding across the Gila Desert to do his dirty work.

For Lope Gamboa, there was no need to hurry.

SEVENTEEN

The Conestoga wagon carrying its load of rifles and government gold was a white prairie schooner adrift on a choppy sea of sand and rock. Like a sailing ship on a sullen swell it rocked lazily over undulations in the terrain to the north of the Mexican border, each lurch causing the canvas cover to flap, each jolt as a wheel dropped into a deep rut wringing a florid curse from the driver.

The escort was riding on the flanks, far enough out to avoid the thick plume of dust kicked up by the wagon wheels and the labouring mules. The dun-coloured cloud rose to hang almost stationary in the hot, still air, slowly drifting as it gained altitude, dissipating only gradually and several miles behind the lumbering wagon. Each of the cavalrymen was aware of the value of the twin cargoes, and that the dust cloud meant Arizonan outlaws or Mexican bandits could track the wagon from a distance and without being seen. So they rode stoically but watchful, sweat glistening on their faces as they turned to scan the skyline, their eyes resentful as, from time to time, they glanced towards the wagon.

A horse was tied to the tailgate. The sergeant was inside the wagon. He was asleep. Even though each lurch of the wagon and each flap of the canvas cooled the air just a little, the heat was unbearable. The sergeant, however, was blissfully unaware. Almost comatose from the previous evening's intake of raw whiskey, he had earlier fallen from the wagon and cracked his head on an inconveniently placed rock. Concussion had been added to the effects of the strong drink, and now he sprawled against the boxes of rifles and snored, his chin wet with spittle.

Hood, Kade and the Coogan brothers rode steadily for most of that day, four men stoically bearing the heat, the dust, and constant debilitating thirst, each man linked to the other three – though in a perilously fragile way – by his lust for gold. They headed across the scorching Gila Desert in a south-easterly direction, knowing that the Conestoga wagon with its military escort would be pushing along the Mexican border and that to cut it off they must choose a precise bearing based on an accurate estimate of the time elapsed and the speed at which the mules could move the wagon. It would be good tactics, they agreed, to arrive at a location that was certain to be on the Conestoga's route, but one it had not yet reached. Between them they had staged two successful ambushes, with no reward. A third, against seasoned military veterans, would prove more difficult, but from it they would not come away empty handed.

All were agreed that the Conestoga wagon was unlikely to cling to the border, much more likely to drift deeper into Arizona and pick up supplies at towns along its route. After a lengthy discussion, several calculations scribbled with a stub of pencil on a scrap of paper and more than one squint up at the sun to gauge direction, they decided that by heading for the settlement of Indian Oasis they would place themselves in a favourable position to set up the ambush before the Conestoga appeared on the horizon. The settlement was midway between Ajo and Nogales, some 150 miles from Yuma, and halfway to the New Mexico border.

It was a gamble but, knowing that they had to choose a destination if they were to intercept the Conestoga, it was towards Indian Oasis that they directed their horses.

They rode with the sun first at their left shoulders, then hot on their faces – in fact, almost directly overhead – then on their right shoulders and gradually cooling as the day drew to a close. When it was a fiery ball on the western horizon, the mountains beneath it little more than distant purple smudges rimmed with gold, they called a halt and made an uneasy camp.

For Lope Gamboa that scorching hot Arizona day was not unpleasant. He had been born in an adobe shack, one of several forming a pueblo sprawled across bare slopes in the blistering heat of northern Sonora. He was accustomed to soaring temperatures. A leather water bag hung from his saddle, its surface glistening. The colourful, broad-brimmed sombrero cast a cooling shadow over his face and shoulders. He wore a loose shirt, and he relaxed and rode with the heat because experience had taught him that fighting it could lead to exhaustion and death.

As Gamboa rode he smoked a thin black cheroot. His eyes, squinting against smoke and sun, were constantly amused, and about him there was an air of quiet confidence.

The four outlaws he followed were not in sight, but for a man of his capabilities the trail they left was like a well-drawn map. He had quickly realized that they were heading for a point somewhere between Yuma and Nogales, and the same shrewdness gave him a clear insight into their intentions. But why should it not? Their intentions and his own were almost identical; it was only in the target that they differed. The four men would ambush the Conestoga wagon; faced with a cavalry escort, it was the only way they could be certain of turning the odds in their favour. With that done, then he, Lope Gamboa, would gun them down. From a distance. One by one.

The thought was exhilarating. His black eyes glittered. He reached down and slid the gleaming Winchester rifle from its boot and worked the lever that slid a bullet from magazine to breech. He lifted the weapon slowly, pressed the butt into his shoulder, rested his unshaven cheek on the stock. Letting his body absorb the movement of his horse so that he was relatively still he drew a bead on a distant saguaro. Very gently, he squeezed the trigger. The crack was brittle, the flight of the bullet a muted whirr, rapidly fading. And, in the far distance, a fragment of green flesh flew from the lofty cactus.

'One down,' Gamboa whispered, his gaze switching to the shimmering horizon beyond which he knew the four riders were pushing on towards the border. 'And then, when the other three are down also – then there is the gold.'

Frank Carson and Joe Creed rode out of Yuma coolly estimating that they faced a ride of at least twenty-four hours before they got close to overtaking the Conestoga wagon. They also had to accept the possibility that the cavalry sergeant might not take the direct route to Fort Huachuca. If he decided to stop off for supplies he could choose any of a number of small towns scattered across Arizona, leaving Carson and Creed floundering in the dust and the heat.

'You got any Injun in your blood?' Carson said, as they left the town of Yuma behind them and headed into the wilderness.

'Strange question,' Creed said.

'Injuns can track,' Carson explained. 'Right now we could do with a man in a breech clout and feathers who could sniff the air, look at a few scratches in the earth and unerringly point us towards that Conestoga.'

'I can follow sign some,' Creed said. 'We know where the wagon was, best thing is to go there, then stay with its tracks.'

'Hmph.' Carson grimaced. 'If we do that we're likely

riding a right angle. Down to the border, then a turn to the east. Save time if we could cut that corner.'

'Sure, but there's no real need,' Creed said. 'It was already heading more east than south when we followed it. We're losing very little by making for its last known position.'

For a few minutes they rode in silence. Then Carson shot Creed a glance.

'If you're right about Gamboa being there, you realize he won't be alone?'

'Of course. There'll be him and the Coogans.'

'That enough to take the cavalry?'

'More than enough if they play it right.'

'So we could get there, and find Gamboa and his pals driving that wagon?'

Creed grinned mirthlessly.

'I'm too nervous to imagine *what* we'll find when we do catch up. I think you're forgetting that what we saw on the Oxbow route indicated two ambushes.'

'Dammit, you're right, I had forgotten,' Carson said softly. 'So, if we factor in those two ex-cons—'

'Adam Kade, Deakin Hood.'

'Right, if we take it for granted they're not going to give up, then we could be heading into a situation unlike anything I've ever encountered.'

'For sure. A couple of hard characters just out of jail, two Irish outlaws and a loco 'breed, all homing in on a military wagon carrying government gold and crates of rifles still packed in factory grease.'

'It's enough to make a man turn his horse and hightail it for home,' Carson said, casting a sly glance in

Creed's direction.

Creed caught the look, and grinned.

'Don't you believe it,' he said. 'All the gold in that wagon wouldn't be enough to keep me away from this battle.'

EIGHTEEN

Twenty-four hours after leaving La Buena Tierra they pulled their weary horses to a halt two miles to the south west of the settlement of Indian Oasis, and looked with considerable misgivings at the one location from which an ambush might be possible.

'Not much choice, even less time,' Mick Coogan said gloomily. 'That dust cloud to the west has got to be the Conestoga wagon, which is something to be thankful for. But where the trail dips and wends its way through that arroyo is surely the only place in a hundred square miles that's going to give us any cover at all.'

'Look on the bright side,' his brother said. 'That wagon's covered something like a hundred and twenty miles in an easterly direction since leaving Yuma, and not once has it been troubled. The escort has been lulled into a sense of security. It's entirely false. We'll wipe them out with straight shooting from the rim of that ravine because they'll come through without bothering to lift their eyes.'

Adam Kade and Deakin Hood were watching and listening. As the quartet had approached Indian Oasis they had deliberately slowed their horses, ensuring that little dust had been raised by their progress. They were confident that, from a distance, the cavalry escort would not have spotted them.

'Between us we should be getting used to this by now,' Hood said. 'We know how the ambush must be worked: two groups of two, in this case to the east and west and some fifty yards apart. When the wagon's in the middle, all four open fire with rifles. Only thing to be settled is who takes up which post, and which targets to aim for.'

Bren Coogan was frowning.

'Not that straightforward. You say you saw two cavalrymen when that wagon left Yuma?'

'That's right. Two soldiers, one spare horse tied to the wagon. Add the driver and shotgun and you've got four men.'

'And where were the two cavalrymen?'

'Outriders. Left and right flank, fifty yards out.'

'That won't work coming through the arroyo, there's no room.'

Hood nodded. 'One soldier will lead the way, the other will take up the rear.'

'You see, that makes it awkward,' Bren Coogan said. 'There is an imbalance: escort, driver and shotgun puts three at the front of the wagon, with just one cavalryman taking up the rear.'

'Then we change our formation,' Mick Coogan said.

137

'Three men positioned to the east, one man to the west to take care of the lone soldier.'

'And be flexible,' Adam Kade warned. 'All this is speculation. We must be prepared for every eventuality.'

'And indeed we will,' Mick Coogan said with a grin. 'We'll spray them with bullets no matter what formation they adopt. In that ravine, or whatever you call that crack in the ground, they'll be caught like rats in a trap.'

The arroyo was a fault formed by the shifting of rock plates deep in the earth. The ancient disturbance had thrown up great ridges in the land for several hundred yards in every direction, with here and there jagged rocky outcrops pointing towards the colourless skies. Mick Coogan appreciated the cover afforded by the irregularity of the terrain but, as he, Bren and Deakin Hood took up their positions at the eastern end of the snaking gully, he knew that good cover could also put them at a disadvantage. If a man hides himself too well, he told Bren, his own field of view is naturally restricted.

'At any other time I would share your concern,' Bren said. 'But this is straightforward.'

'So you've quickly changed your tune? Didn't I hear you say it was awkward?'

'Ah, yes, but didn't we then work it out to our satisfaction?'

'Only the result will tell us if it's satisfactory or not,' Mick said.

'Well, that won't be long in coming. If you look now

you'll see the wagon's already entering the western end of the arroyo.'

Hood, who had opted to team up with the Coogans at the eastern end of the arroyo and tackle the Conestoga head on, was only half listening as he squinted into the distance.

'That run down into the arroyo must be a pig for driver and mules,' he said. 'The wagon's dipping and rocking, canvas flapping like a tent in a storm. It's also kicking up dust like nobody's business.'

'The soldier taking up the rear will be eating it,' Mick Coogan said. 'I wonder if the two of them drew straws?'

Bren Coogan was moving through the rocks to the rim of the arroyo.

'Time to put ourselves where we can see but not be seen,' he called. 'There's three of us, and three of them. Play it right, we fire three shots and it's all over.'

'Then it's down to Kade,' Hood said, and he shaded his eyes with his hands in an effort to catch a glimpse of his partner. 'He's well hidden, facing a lone cavalryman who's behind the wagon and spitting dust. Be like shooting a blind man.'

He had walked after Bren Coogan, his boots slipping on the uneven surface. At the rim he followed Mick Coogan's example and took up a position in the rocks that gave him a clear view down the length of the arroyo. All three men were holding Winchesters. Bren Coogan was sitting cross-legged, using his knees as supports for his elbows. Hood again copied Mick Coogan and stretched out on his belly. His right hand was on the rifle's pistol grip, holding the weapon snug into his shoulder. His left hand, supporting the rifle barrel, was resting on a boulder.

'Here's a thought,' Mick Coogan said. 'It's possible the soldier riding in front of the wagon could be leading it by some distance. That puts too much space between the targets.'

'Then we let him ride on by,' Hood said, thinking it through. 'If you're right, I'll track him all the way through with my rifle. When you two cut down the driver and shotgun, I'll shoot that lead soldier when he swings round to see what's going on.'

Nods of agreement. A heavy silence.

Hood could hear the other two men breathing harshly, rapidly, and he knew they were feeling the mounting tension. Then out of the silence he heard the first faint creaking and rattling that announced the Conestoga's approach.

'That's it,' Bren said, and he levered a shell into his rifle's breech. 'That's what we've been waiting for.'

'Easy now,' Mick Coogan said softly. 'When it's in sight, the situation we see before us will dictate when we must open fire. But let me say now that I'll be the one to take the driver. Bren, you take the guard. Hood, you've already said you'll take care of the escort, whether he's close to the wagon or away in front.'

'To echo your brother's earlier sentiments,' Hood said, squinting down the arroyo, 'it's not going to be quite that straightforward. I can see the lead mules now. But if I can see the mules, then where's the escort?'

'Ah, don't worry about it, it was only our opinion that they would—'

Mick broke off and strained to look into the distance as a shot cracked out. It came from somewhere down the arroyo. Hood judged the source to be beyond the approaching Conestoga which was now in full view, rocking crazily as the snorting mules pulled it over the rutted ground.

'Dammit,' Bren said fiercely, 'Kade's started it too soon.'

'That was a handgun, not a rifle,' Mick said. 'A handgun's for close work.'

'Then he's hit trouble,' Hood said.

'Trouble's hit him, more like—'

And again Mick Coogan broke off abruptly. This time he was interrupted, not by a shot, but by a snapped command.

'Drop your rifles, all three of you, then stand up and put your hands on your heads.'

Some twenty yards behind them, half hidden by the tall rocks that rose in slabbed steps from the arroyo's rim, a mounted cavalry trooper was covering them with a Sharps carbine.

Mick Coogan grinned. Still lying down he twisted around, deliberately held his rifle vertically with the butt resting on rock.

'A single-shot weapon,' he said to the sweating trooper, 'and there's three of us. Now there's a fine predicament to be in.'

'One of you dies if I pull the trigger,' the trooper said. 'It's not me who's facing a difficult decision.'

He was still looking at Mick Coogan when Bren Coogan spun on his knees and triggered his rifle. The shot was wild. It smacked into the cavalry horse and brought it down to its knees and out into the open. It began to fall sideways, eyes glazing. The trooper kicked his feet from the stirrups and threw himself towards the rocks. Bren Coogan fired again. Hood spun into a sitting position and opened fire. Splinters flew from the rocks. Ricochets howled into the hot air.

But the trooper made it into cover.

The horse flopped onto its side, and died. Mick Coogan came up on one knee, his face livid.

'It's all falling apart,' he said. 'The other trooper must have downed Adam Kade, otherwise there would have been more than one shot—'

'Quit talking, and start shooting,' Bren burst out. 'Those shots have warned the driver. He's whipping those mules and they'll be past us.'

Hood had already recognized the danger. The Conestoga's driver was standing with legs braced, traces in one hand, whip in the other. It was curling back, then streaking out over the mules and cracking close to the leader's ears. Already the wagon, twenty feet below them in the arroyo, was drawing level with the bushwhackers.

Hood lifted his rifle, slammed it into his shoulder and fired twice. His first shot took the driver in the throat. He dropped the whip and fell back, spouting blood.

The guard was already lifting and swinging his shotgun. He pulled the trigger. Buckshot screamed past Hood, plucking at his shirt as he ducked back.

Then Mick Coogan joined the fray. As the wagon

lurched by he stepped forward, took careful aim with his rifle and pulled the trigger. The guard spotted him. Mouth open beneath his drooping moustache, eyes wide, he pulled the shotgun's second trigger. But it was an instinctive, dying reaction. Mick Coogan's bullet had drilled into his chest. The guard was already falling backwards off the wagon's boot when the shotgun's second barrel sent buckshot screaming harmlessly skywards.

With the driver no longer tormenting them with the whip and the way out of the arroyo growing ever steeper, the mules drew to a halt. The wagon began to roll backwards. Then one of the rear wheels dropped into a deep rut. Canted to one side, the Conestoga rocked, then became still. The spare horse tied to tailgate stood quivering, its ears flat to its skull.

'One job done and two men down,' Mick Coogan said, turning away from the carnage, 'but now there's the other two to deal with and they'll be a different proposition.'

'We know where one is,' Bren said, 'and if Kade's down then the other will be coming this way.'

'Then there's no use staying bunched. What we must do—'

Whatever came next was lost to Deakin Hood. He caught a movement out of the corner of his eye. It came from the far side of the rocks where the cavalry mount lay with flies already buzzing around its head. All Hood saw was a quick flash of a cavalry jacket, buttons gleaming in the sun. Then came the gleam of a rifle barrel, the spurt of flame from the muzzle.

143

Deakin Hood saw no more, and heard nothing. The bullet hit him in the temple. He was dead before he hit the ground.

NINETEEN

It was some time after midday, with the sun a physical weight bearing down on their shoulders and the dust and sweat an irritating, itching presence on just about every inch of their skin, when Joe Creed flicked a glance at Frank Carson.

'Hear that?'

'Well, either my ears are popping, or someone is doing some shooting.'

'We know the Conestoga's out there. If it's being attacked, we could be too late.'

'To catch Gamboa?' Carson shrugged, then spat drily. 'Everything we've done is based on speculation. All we can do is keep going and hope you're wrong.'

'True, but we need to change direction,' Creed said. 'Those shots came from a position some way to the north of where we're heading. The heat-haze makes a mess of visibility, but it seems to me that there's some rock formations out that way – which makes just about the only change of scenery in more than half a day.'

'And a good spot for an ambush?'

'Let's go see.'

Fifteen minutes later, and the dark specks that were vultures began circling over the smudge of higher ground. After another half-hour Carson and Creed were still riding a recognizable trail, yet approaching an area of jagged rocky outcrops that seemed to prevent any further progress in that direction. It was only when they drew much nearer that they realized the trail ran straight towards those rocks, then turned sharply and entered an arroyo.

'If I was a bushwhacker,' Carson said, 'I'd be hard pressed to find a better spot.'

Creed grunted. His eyes were on the circling scavengers, his face grim. Feeling vulnerable, feeling that tingling in the spine that always comes when death could come from a single rifle shot out of the blue nowhere, they rode down the rock slope into the arroyo. The sound of their horses' hoofs rang against the rocky walls. For a short while it seemed as if the ancient fissure would close in on them, ruling out any possibility that the Conestoga wagon had passed that way. But in the next quarter mile it gradually widened, the shadows that had brought a breath of welcome coolness retreated, and once more they were riding in the heat of the midday sun.

But not for long.

Some way ahead both men saw where the ruts, both ancient and more recent, had been badly torn and churned. The marks left by wagon wheels were easily recognizable.

'Conestoga got into trouble right there, and sort of

slid to a messy halt,' Carson said emphatically. 'And I reckon those shiny bits I can see glittering in the dust are spent shells.'

'That's not all,' Creed said. 'Look, over there in those rocks.'

Even as he pointed, a vulture rose from the ground and flapped away, its powerful wings carrying it over the arroyo's rim.

'Goddammit,' Carson said. 'No need to ask what we'll find over there. Question is, who is it, and who did the killing?'

His jaw was tight as he swung his horse towards the rocky walls. The animal was already skittish at the smell of blood, trying to pull back, its ears flat. Carson held it on a tight rein, rode it a few more yards then swung down from the saddle. He left the reins trailing, hoping the horse wouldn't bolt, but more concerned with what he would find. He was aware of Creed following him, but all his attention was focused on what he could see half hidden behind a heap of boulders.

'Jesus,' he said softly.

He crunched around the rocks, put a hand against the warm cliff face as he gazed down on three, four – no, dammit, there were *five* bodies there, a gruesome heap of once living flesh where now blowflies buzzed and already there was evidence that several of the circling vultures had been down to the carnage, ripping and tearing with sharp beaks.

'Two old-timers,' Creed said.

He'd brushed past Carson and reached down to grab clothing and pull the bodies apart.

'They'll be the coach driver and guard,' Carson said.

'And the other three?'

'Best we can do is guess,' Carson said, his voice thick and clogged. 'Gamboa's not in that heap of dead flesh. Two could be the Coogans, the other one of their gang, or maybe Kade or Hood.'

'So what the hell happened here?'

Carson leaned back against the cliff face, took off his hat and fanned his face.

'The Conestoga's not here, so it kept going. Only way I can explain what we've got is the wagon was ambushed and the first shots took the driver and guard. But we know there were three seasoned cavalrymen with that wagon. Looks to me like after the initial shock they got the better of the outlaws, dumped the bodies here and moved off in a hell of a hurry.'

'Yeah, that figures. In a normal situation they would have taken time to cover them with rocks to keep off the animals and those damn vultures.' Creed looked steadily at Carson. 'What about Gamboa?'

Carson shook his head.

'I pointed out earlier that we've been relying on speculation. We're still doing it. We're looking at five dead men. The only sure way of finding out what happened to them – and if Lope Gamboa was involved – is to go after the Conestoga and talk to the soldiers.'

'All right,' Creed said, 'let's do that. But we'd better make sure we approach with extreme caution. From what we've seen here, if those soldiers think we're a second bunch of owlhoots we might not live to see another day.'

*

It was soon evident from the tracks they followed when they rode out of the arroyo that the man driving the Conestoga wagon was finding the going difficult. With the coach driver murdered it had to be one of the soldiers doing the driving, and several times the wagon had veered off the trail. There were also clear signs that it had been forced to pull up more than once, and Carson and Creed took heart from the knowledge that such delays meant they must be closing fast.

But were they closing fast enough to catch up with the wagon before Gamboa struck?

The landscape had changed again, and now they were riding to the south of a long, barren ridge where a few lofty saguaros were outlined against searing skies that were almost white. They had for some time been aware of the dust cloud hanging just a few miles ahead of them. After half an hour's hard riding they could see the wagon's white canvas at the heart of the cloud; another fifteen minutes and the creak and rattle of the wagon and the squealing of its tortured wheels could be heard even above the thunder of their horses' hoofs, and at the same time, they caught their first glimpse of the horse tied to the tailgate and the two outriders dressed in cavalry blue.

'Still half a mile away, but we can see them and if they look back they'll see us,' Carson said. 'Let's make sure they can see us real well when we get close, so no bad mistakes are made.'

149

Creed, his eyes intent on the rocking Conestoga wagon and its escort, nodded agreement.

'I'd hate to get shot by the good guys just when I'm getting close to Gamboa.'

'Yeah, and I'd hate it if we were basing all our hopes on wild speculation that's going to prove worthless,' Carson said.

The words had no sooner left his lips than one of the cavalrymen riding at the edge of the dust cloud toppled out of the saddle. His boot caught in the stirrup as he went down. He hit the ground with his shoulders and, as the horse took off and dragged the man across the rocky ground, the crack of a rifle shot rang out. In the same instant, the rider on the far side of the Conestoga flung up his arms, then fell backwards. He bounced off the horse's rump, hit the ground hard and lay still. The sharp report of the shot that had drilled into his back came fractions of a second later.

Carson pulled his horse to a halt and cast a grim glance towards Creed.

'The time between those slugs hitting and the sound of the shots puts that gunman some way away.'

'Which makes him an excellent marksman,' Creed said. 'Tell me, what do we know about Gamboa?'

'That's part of it: I hear he can shoot flies off an apple without breaking the skin.'

'Then riding close to that wagon now is too dangerous. We should stay well back and watch developments.'

While talking, Creed was standing in the stirrups, his

eyes searching the horizon away to the north.

'The shots came from that direction. He's firing from a position on that ridge, maybe close to those big organ pipes.'

'The driver will have worked that out,' Carson said. 'He's a military man. If he had any sense he'd be pointing that rig towards the south and running for his life—'

'Grounds too rough,' Creed said. 'He's forced to stay on the trail.'

'Then he's a sitting duck, and he needs our help.'

'No, wait—'

'To hell with that.'

Gritting his teeth, Carson used the end of the reins to whip his horse from standstill to a fast gallop. With the wind flattening his hat brim he closed in on the lurching Conestoga. As he entered the drifting cloud of dust he raced past the bodies of the cavalrymen and the riderless horses that had come together and now stood quivering. Even as he rode in at a furious, reckless pace the wagon's driver attempted to take evasive action: he stood up on the box and, even from a distance, Carson could see him hauling on the traces as he tried to bring the Conestoga round and turn its rear end to the distant gunman.

He almost made it.

As Carson watched in horror, the man standing on the box arched his back in an agonizing spasm, his face turned towards the dazzling skies. Then the crack of the shot caught up with the bullet that had already snapped his spine. As it did so, one of the wagon's front wheels struck a boulder. The Conestoga bounced high. The the dying man was thrown from the box. He seemed to hang in the air. Then he hit the ground, flopped too close to the wagon and a rear wheel ran over him with an audible crunch.

Within ten yards the mule team had come to a halt. Coated with white lather, steaming in the hot, dry air, they stood with ears flattened as the Conestoga creaked to a halt behind them.

Creed rode up behind Carson.

'I warned you to hang back,' he said. 'If that's Gamboa, he's done all he figured was necessary to leave that government gold there for the taking. But now we've upset the apple-cart. From that high vantage point he'll have seen us ride in and he'll be cursing because suddenly there's two more men to deal with—'

'Men of a different calibre—'

'He'll pick us off from a distance. The only cover we've got is this wagon. We're pinned down.'

Carson grinned savagely.

'So's he, if you think about it. This is a classic Mexican stand-off. The gold's here. Gamboa's up there on the ridge. To reach that gold he's got to cross a good half mile of open ground, and that's something he can't risk.'

'Then he'll wait for darkness.'

'And if he does, he'll hand us the advantage. Two defenders under cover able to take turns at keeping watch, one weary man advancing across open ground.'

Suddenly Creed's eyes were glinting.

'How's it go in the army, two hours on, four off?' He grinned and drew a coin from his pocket. 'I'll toss you for first stag.'

TWENTY

Lope Gamboa came down from the ridge when, by Carson's turnip watch, it was two hours after midnight. Since deciding that Gamboa would wait for darkness to make his move the two men had done nothing to make their presence known. They'd surmised that Gamboa had watched them bear down on the Conestoga as the last of the cavalrymen was shot in the back, but in the faint hope that they had slipped through the dust cloud without being noticed they made sure they kept the wagon's bulk between them and the distant gunman. Regretfully, keeping the deception going meant leaving the horse tethered to the tailgate, and the mule team standing in the traces. Cruel, yes, but Carson reckoned the end justified the means and, as he pointed out, the temperature dropped as night approached and the animals' suffering would be relieved.

Creed was on watch. Carson was dozing under the wagon, and he came awake instantly as the tall man bent and touched his shoulder.

'He's coming in on the east side,' he said softly. 'That

will bring him in around or through the mules. That's crafty. He's figuring if we hear a sound we'll put it down to the mules getting restless. Also, if he comes straight through them we'll be pushed to get a clear shot.'

Carson rolled clear of the wagon and stood up. A pale moon was casting its eerie light over the desert. Creed's face was animated, his eyes gleaming with an unpleasant, killing fervour.

'How close?' Carson said.

'He's almost on us.'

Swiftly Carson drew his six-gun. Creed had already moved along the side of the Conestoga. His back was flattened against the boards, his six-gun held high as he looked towards the mules who were in the traces and asleep on their feet.

And now Carson caught the sound of the approaching horse. Yet even as the faint crunch of hoofs on the hard packed desert earth reached his ears he sensed something was wrong. The horse was coming down from the ridge at a canter when Carson would have expected a silent, furtive approach. Gamboa was a cunning man, a renegade experienced in fighting dirty. A man such as he would never ride head on into danger. All right, there was the faint possibility that he'd been so proud of his marksmanship when downing the soldiers that he hadn't seen Carson and Creed approach the Conestoga, but Carson knew that was unlikely. Which meant, Carson reasoned, that Gamboa knew exactly what he was doing, and that what Carson was hearing was something he was meant to hear, something—

'Creed,' he whispered urgently, 'get back here, that horse is a diversion and Gamboa's coming on foot.'

Even then, even though he moved as soon as realization hit home and he'd issued the warning, he was almost too late.

As he watched Creed swing around in surprise, Carson heard the horse at the tailgate whicker softly. Without thinking, he turned and dropped to one knee. He was down but off balance, one hand reaching for the wagon, when a muzzle flash lit up the night. The light was blinding. The crack of the six-gun came from mere yards away. A bullet whistled over his head. With red blotches ruining his vision, Carson fired blindly. He fired at a point a fraction to the right of the second muzzle flash that sent a bullet hissing close to his ear. As he did so he heard a grunt, then the heavy, unmistakable sound of a body hitting the ground.

'You got him,' Creed said.

He brushed past Carson, but Carson thrust out an arm to hold him back. Then, together they went to the downed gunman.

Gamboa had already heaved himself up so that his back was against a wagon wheel. His sombrero had slipped sideways. His streaked grey hair glistened in the moonlight. He had both hands pressed to his middle, where his shirt was soaked with blood.

'You downed three cavalrymen,' Creed said, 'and I guess you thought we'd be just as easy, but you were wrong.'

Gamboa was grinning. 'Maybe so, but you two got everything wrong,' he said. 'The men I shot here, with

156

my rifle, they are not soldiers. The two on horseback were the Coogan brothers, the other a man from the jail, a man called Adam Kade. I watched them ambush those soldiers, then don their clothing. They killed them, every one, but another man who was released from jail, he died.'

'Deakin Hood or Adam Kade,' Creed said.

But Gamboa, knowing he was dying, was not listening.

'It was clever, the way it was planned by them, the way it was planned by me,' he said hoarsely. 'And it would have worked, goddammit it was working, I almost had my hands on that gold—'

'Except I turned up,' Joe Creed said, 'a man from the past. You murdered my family fifteen years ago, you and a bunch of no good Indians. . . .'

And then his voice trailed off. Gamboa's eyes were open, but unseeing. Life had left the renegade's body. Gamboa was dead.

'I guess it ends here,' Frank Carson said quietly. He reached down, and with the tips of two fingers he closed the 'breed's eyes. 'The hunt for Lope Gamboa's over, and I can't say I'm sorry. The men who murdered my partner have paid the price, though not by my hand which I suppose is something to be thankful for. As for you, well, I guess you must feel some satisfaction – but in a way you've been frustrated in your quest for justice, so is the way this finished up enough to put an end to your grieving?'

'Oh, that part is,' Joe Creed said.

He was leaning against the side of the wagon with the

appearance of nonchalance, but something in the man's tone put Carson on his guard.

'As you've already made clear to me,' Creed went on, 'when my family died a lot of blame lay with the Texas Rangers. So the hunt for Gamboa may be over, but for me it doesn't end there.'

'Jesus Christ,' Frank Carson said.

He was staring into the muzzle of Joe Creed's six-gun.

'You're kidding, right? This is some kind of joke?'

'No joke,' Creed said. 'A lot of people died on my parents' farm, a lot of people did the killing, directly or indirectly.'

He stopped talking, a frown creasing his brow. The Conestoga wagon had rocked. Not enough to knock Creed off balance, though all his weight was on it, but the movement itself had come as a shock and destroyed his concentration. His eyes wavered. The gun in his hand drooped.

Frank Carson stepped back and lifted his own six-gun.

The movement brought back Creed's awareness. As if mentally shaking himself, he jerked around. The two men faced each other, less than six feet apart. Like men moving with a weight on their shoulders they fought to bring their six-guns level. Two fingers pressed two triggers. Two shots rang out. Muzzle flashes again lit the desert air.

Creed's bullet kicked up the dirt between Carson's boots. The Texas Ranger's bullet hit Creed between the eyes. A black hole appeared, welled dark blood. The tall

158

man rocked backwards. His head cracked against the side of the Conestoga. His knees buckled and slid down to a sitting position. He came to rest alongside Lope Gamboa, then toppled sideways until he was leaning on the dead 'breed.

For a long moment there was absolute silence.

Then a new voice spoke up.

'A pretty picture,' the cavalry sergeant said. He dropped down from the Conestoga and stood swaying. His eyes were swollen and bloodshot. There was a huge purple lump on his forehead, and his hands shook as he dragged the makings from his pocket and began rolling a cigarette.

'If you've been in there all this time,' Carson said in disbelief, 'you must have slept the clock around.'

'What the hell else is there to do crossing the Gila Desert 'cept drink and sleep?' the sergeant said. 'I've got good men in my troop, they know their job and do it—'

He broke off, looking around him in comical bewilderment.

'Where the hell are my men?' he said, almost plaintively.

Carson sighed.

'Soldier, the best thing we can do is get a fire going, brew some coffee to clear your head,' he said. 'It's a long, complicated story, but I reckon by the time we're finished you'll admit it's the best camp-fire yarn you've heard in a long time.'